FROM THE NANCY DREW FILES

THE CASE: Wedding preparations are in full swing . . . but Nancy's preparing for danger.

CONTACT: Nancy's old friend Angela has designed her own gown, but someone's coming dressed to kill.

SUSPECTS: Raphael Marino—*Did Angela's fiancé try to kill his old girlfriend, Shannon, in order to shut her up?*

Glenn MacInnes—*Did jealousy drive Shannon's boyfriend over the edge . . . to the point of attempted murder?*

Angela Chamberlain—*Did the bride herself set out to destroy the one person who could destroy her happiness?*

COMPLICATIONS: Jealousy. Greed. Deception. Can love conquer all? Or will crime win out? Nancy's determined to save a marriage . . . before the wedding vows have even been spoken!

Books in The Nancy Drew Files® Series

Available from ARCHWAY Paperbacks

The Nancy Drew Files™ 118

BETRAYED BY LOVE

CAROLYN KEENE

AN ARCHWAY PAPERBACK
Published by POCKET BOOKS
New York London Toronto Sydney Tokyo Singapore

This book is a work of fiction. Names, characters, places and incidents are products of the author's imagination or are used fictitiously. Any resemblance to actual events or locales or persons, living or dead, is entirely coincidental.

AN ARCHWAY PAPERBACK *Original*

An Archway Paperback published by
POCKET BOOKS, a division of Simon & Schuster Inc.
1230 Avenue of the Americas, New York, NY 10020

ISBN: 0-671-56876-0

First Archway Paperback printing December 1996

10 9 8 7 6 5 4 3 2 1

Printed in the U.S.A.

IL 6+

BETRAYED
BY LOVE

Chapter

One

WHERE HAVE YOU BEEN, George? I was about to hang up—the phone must have rung a dozen times," Nancy Drew said in response to George Fayne's breathless "Hello?"

"It shouldn't take a hotshot detective like you long to figure that out," George teased. "I was running, of course. I always run on Saturdays."

Nancy glanced out the window. The freezing rain made the late November morning seem more like a day in midwinter. "I know, but I thought that in this weather you'd stay home."

Her friend snorted. "No way! Got to keep in shape if I want to win the Holiday Marathon next month like last year. So what's up?"

"I was wondering if you'd like to come over for lunch today," Nancy said. "I just spoke to Bess, and she's coming."

"Sure, why not? You want us to help finish the leftover turkey from Thanksgiving, right?"

Laughing, Nancy said, "You got it. Dad's completely turkeyed out, and anyway, he left for Seattle yesterday. The Steinbeck trial starts next week, you know."

"Everybody knows," George said. "There have been dozens of articles about it in the paper—'River Heights Attorney Carson Drew for the Defense,' stuff like that. Is the trial going to be covered by Court TV?"

"I doubt it," Nancy replied. "This isn't a celebrity murder trial or anything. Now let's get back to lunch. Hannah said she'd make her famous turkey tetrazzini if I could round up a crew to help me eat it." Hannah Gruen was the Drews' housekeeper, and a wonderful cook.

"What about Ned?" George asked, referring to Nancy's boyfriend, Ned Nickerson. "Have you invited him? That guy's a bottomless pit. He could take care of that leftover problem all by himself."

"You're probably right," Nancy agreed. "But unfortunately Ned took off on a skiing trip with some of his buddies from college."

"Really? How come you didn't go with him?"

Nancy shrugged. "He didn't ask me. I got the impression this trip is a guy thing—male bonding, or some important thing like that. So it'll be just you, Bess, and me."

"Okay. I'll pick Bess up on the way. What time should we show up?"

"How about twelve-thirty?" Nancy suggested.

"Sounds good. I've already worked up an appetite. By then I'll be starving."

"Listen, there's another reason I want you two to come over, though," Nancy added. "I got a letter from Angela Chamberlain today, and she sent her designs for her wedding gown and my bridesmaid's dress. I'm dying to show them to you both! They're really gorgeous. Angela's making mine of poinsettia red velvet, to carry out the Christmas theme, and hers will be snow white brocade."

"Velvet and brocade?" George echoed. "You're gushing, Nancy, and that's not like you. It sounds as though you're coming down with a bad case of wedding fever. Has Ned caught it, too? Are the two of you going to be the next bride and groom?"

"Oh, please!" Nancy protested. "I am *not* gushing, and neither of us has wedding fever. I'm going to be Angela's bridesmaid, and Ned's going to be a groomsman, and that's absolutely all there is to it!"

George laughed. "Okay, okay! Forget I mentioned it. See you at twelve-thirty, Nan."

As Nancy hung up the phone in her room, she glanced at Angela's sketches again. There was no doubt about it: A Christmas wedding was very romantic. For a brief moment she pictured herself in the bridal gown and veil, with a beaming Ned at her side.

Maybe I do have just a touch of wedding fever, she admitted to herself and smiled. But I'm not going to tell George—she'll never let me forget it!

A few hours later Nancy's two best friends arrived at her house.

"This weather is the total pits," Bess Marvin grumbled as she and George took off their wet jackets. She looked at her reflection in the hall mirror, then pulled a comb out of her shoulder bag and tugged it through her damp blond hair. "Yuck! Nice hairdo, eh? Good thing I have an appointment at Hair Dimensions later this afternoon. I have a date with Walt tonight, and if he saw me looking like this, he'd never ask me out again!"

George grinned at her. "Sure he would. Don't be such a ditz, Bess. When I was running this morning, I passed Walt on the track. He's pretty cool. A little thing like a bad hair day wouldn't turn him off."

Looking from tall, athletic George in her bright blue sweats to petite, feminine Bess in snug designer jeans and a fuzzy pink sweater,

Nancy commented, "The two of you are so different that sometimes I find it hard to believe you're cousins! Come on into the living room. You can dry off by the fire and look at Angela's drawings until lunch is ready."

When Bess and George were comfortably settled in front of the fireplace, Nancy brought out the sketches and passed them around.

"I love them!" Bess exclaimed. "Angela's a lot more talented than I thought. The style is so elegant, with that portrait neckline and full skirt. You'll look terrific in the bridesmaid's gown, Nancy. It takes somebody tall like you or George to carry it off. Good thing Angela didn't ask *me* to be a bridesmaid. I'd probably look like a red mushroom in that dress."

Nancy laughed. "You would not! Angela's even shorter than you, Bess, and she certainly wouldn't design a dress that made *her* look like a mushroom on her wedding day."

Sitting back in her chair, George ran a hand through her short, dark curls. "To tell the truth, I'm kind of surprised that Angela's getting married at all. Let's face it. When the Chamberlains lived in River Heights, the guys weren't exactly standing in line to ask her out."

"That's for sure," Bess said.

"I didn't know Angela very well—hardly anybody did except you and Ned, Nancy,"

5

George went on. "Most of the kids thought she was stuck-up because her father was so wealthy, but she just struck me as being awfully shy."

Bess nodded. "Especially around boys. I don't remember Angela ever having a date. I bet she could have, though, if she'd just fixed herself up a little. She didn't dress like other girls, either—she always wore those funky clothes she designed."

"Hey, remember, the only thing she's ever really cared about is fashion design," Nancy pointed out. "In fact, she squeezed four years of design classes into three. Obviously she wasn't a total workaholic, though. She found time to meet Rafe Marino, her fiancé, while she was at the art institute. He's in the fine arts program."

Nancy was proud of her friend Angela and what she had accomplished. She had recently graduated with honors from the Manhattan Institute of Art and Design. She had enrolled at the school three years earlier when her father, Gordon Chamberlain, relocated the corporate headquarters of Galaxy Computers from Chicago to New York and moved his family to Soundview, the estate he had purchased on Long Island's exclusive North Shore.

A year later Mr. Chamberlain had died suddenly from a massive heart attack. It had been a terrible shock for Angela, but Howard Tremain,

Gordon's business partner and a close friend of the family, had been a constant source of comfort and support to Angela and her mother, Felicia. No one was particularly surprised when less than a year after Gordon died, Felicia and Howard were married.

Bess heaved a sigh. "Rafe, short for Raphael—it's such a romantic name, absolutely perfect for an artist. And you told us he actually grew up only a few miles away from Soundview. It seems like fate, doesn't it?"

George raised an eyebrow. "I don't know about that, Bess. Sounds more like good planning to me."

"Good planning? What are you talking about?" Nancy asked, frowning.

George shrugged. "Consider the facts. According to you, this guy is on a full scholarship, which means he doesn't have any money. Everybody in the area where he lives must know how super-rich Angela's family is. When Mr. Chamberlain died, it was probably common knowledge that his only child stood to inherit big bucks on her twenty-first birthday— news like that travels fast in a small town. And Angela is twenty now, right? When Rafe marries her and she turns twenty-one, he'll be set for life."

"George, you are so cynical!" Bess chided. *"I*

think it's very romantic. Of course, it's sad that Angela doesn't have her father to give her away, but—"

Nancy interrupted. "That's true, but she gets along really well with her stepfather, so he's walking her down the aisle."

"That's great," Bess said. "He must be pretty special since he's flying you and Ned to New York in his private jet."

Nancy nodded. "First-class all the way."

Bess sighed. "I am so jealous. Angela's wedding will probably be *the* social event of the season on Long Island."

"It'll probably make the front page of every newspaper on the East Coast," George said dryly. Turning to Nancy, she asked, "So, how many bridesmaids and groomsmen will there be besides you and Ned? Ten? Twenty?"

Nancy laughed. "None," she said. "We're it."

"You're kidding!" Bess exclaimed. "I thought Angela's wedding would be like a Charles and Diana rerun, with dozens of attendants!"

George gave her a look. "Yeah, right. And you know how well *that* turned out."

"It's going to be a very small wedding because Angela's mother hasn't been well lately," Nancy told them. "Mrs. Chamberlain—I mean Mrs. Tremain—definitely isn't up to making arrangements for the extravaganza she'd originally planned. That's okay with Angela, though.

She never wanted a big wedding in the first place, but she was willing to go along with it to please her mother."

"What's wrong with Angela's mom?" George asked.

"I don't know. Neither does Angela," Nancy replied. "Apparently nobody does, not even Mrs. Tremain's doctors. They've been running all sorts of tests, but nothing conclusive has shown up. She's just very weak and tired, and Angela says she's lost a lot of weight. She hardly eats anything because her stomach is upset all the time."

"Gee, that's too bad. My aunt Ruth had the very same symptoms, and it turned out that she had an ulcer," George volunteered. "Maybe that's Mrs. Tremain's problem, too."

"Well, there's nothing wrong with *my* stomach except hunger pangs," Bess joked. "I'm surprised you can't hear it growling, 'Feed me, feed me!' That turkey smells delicious. When do we eat?"

Hannah Gruen marched into the living room. "Any minute now, if Nancy ever gets around to making the salad," she said, winking at Bess and George.

"Oops!" Nancy leaped to her feet. "Sorry about that, Hannah. We've been talking about Angela Chamberlain's wedding, and I completely forgot about everything else."

Hannah shook her head. "I feel so sorry for that poor girl, with her father dead, her mother sick, and her fiancé a fortune hunter."

"Oh, Hannah, give me a break." Nancy laughed. "You sound like George. Just because Angela's an heiress doesn't mean that Rafe is marrying her for her money."

"It doesn't mean he isn't, either," Hannah said. "Remember when the heiress to the Fontaine fortune was murdered on her honeymoon and her new husband was the prime suspect?"

Nancy rolled her eyes. "Of course I remember," she said. "Dad was the attorney for the defense. He proved that the husband was innocent. What does that have to do with Angela and Rafe?"

"Well, nothing, I guess," the housekeeper admitted. "But if anything should happen to Angela after they're married, who stands to benefit? Rafe Marino, I bet!"

Nancy stared at her. "Hannah, what's gotten into you? We have no reason to believe Rafe is anything other than a perfectly kind and loving guy. And you've already got him in the murder lineup."

"I just can't stop thinking about that Fontaine case, that's all." Hannah put her hands on her hips. "Now, are you going to make that salad or what?"

"I'll do it right now. Turkey à la Hannah and salad à la Nancy coming right up," Nancy promised.

"I'll give you a hand," George offered.

"Me, too," said Bess.

They followed Hannah into the kitchen, where Nancy made the dressing, Bess washed and dried the greens, and George sliced cucumbers and tomatoes.

When Hannah took the casserole out of the oven and carried it into the dining room, Bess said, "I can't believe that Hannah thinks Angela's in danger from Rafe. *You* don't believe it, do you, Nancy?"

Nancy smiled. "Of course not. Hannah's been with us so long that she tends to see everything as a case to be solved."

"So, where are Angela and Rafe going on their honeymoon?" George asked.

"Paris first, then the south of France." Nancy poured the dressing over the greens and tossed the salad. "They'll stay there for a while, and then spend another few months in Italy so Rafe can study art and Angela can hook up with some designers in Milan. They'll probably be gone for about a year."

"Wow!" Bess breathed. "Most newlyweds just get a week."

"True, but Angela and Rafe are different

from most newlyweds," George said. "They'll have all the time in the world, and plenty of money—*Angela's* money."

Nancy frowned at her. "Why do you keep trashing Rafe, George? Angela's crazy in love with him. Don't you want her to be happy?"

"Sure I do. I'm not trashing Rafe. I just hope for Angela's sake that he's in love with *her,* not with the mega-bucks she's going to inherit!"

Chapter

Two

BRRR! I'm freezing to death!" Nancy said to her boyfriend, Ned Nickerson. "I've had it with skating." Her teeth chattering, she added, "I could do with some hot chocolate. Let's go back to my house, okay? We can make popcorn and warm up in front of the fire."

Grinning, Ned pulled her close and planted a kiss on her cold nose. "Sounds good to me. I've been freezing for hours, but I didn't want to wimp out on you."

"And I've been toughing it out because I didn't want you to think *I'm* a wimp! Thanks, Nickerson." Nancy gave him a playful punch on the arm. "You're a real pal."

"I hope I'm more than a pal," Ned said softly as they glided hand in hand across the ice on

Potter's Pond to a bench on the snowy bank where they had left their boots.

Nancy smiled up at him, thinking, as she often did, how handsome he was. "Better believe it!"

As they sat down on the bench and unlaced their skates, Ned asked, "Then you're not still mad at me for going on that ski trip without you last weekend?"

"I was never mad at you, Ned. I told you that when you called me from school this week. I mean, we're not Siamese twins. You do your thing and I do mine." Nancy massaged her frozen feet before slipping them into her boots. "As a matter of fact, I hardly missed you at all. I had a great time while you were gone."

Ned frowned. "You did?"

"Yeah. I had a real heavy date on Saturday," Nancy teased. Before he could explode, she added, laughing, "With Bess and George. They came over for lunch that afternoon, and I showed them Angela's designs for her wedding gown and my bridesmaid's dress. Good thing you weren't there. You would have been bored to tears with all the wedding talk. You definitely wouldn't have been bored by lunch, though. We had Hannah's turkey tetrazzini."

"Now I really *am* jealous," Ned said. "The skiing was terrific, but the food at the ski lodge was awful."

Ned stood up and pulled Nancy to her feet. "I guess I'll have to settle for a consolation prize. Time for that hot chocolate and popcorn. Let's go!"

Carrying their skates, they trudged through the snow to the lot where Nancy had parked her blue Mustang. She slid behind the wheel, and fifteen minutes later they arrived at the Drews' house.

Hannah met them at the door. "Nancy, Angela Chamberlain phoned a few minutes ago," she said. "She wants you to call her back. It's important, she said."

Nancy slipped out of her turquoise jacket and hung it up in the hall closet. "I'll call her right away. While I'm on the phone, would you mind making some hot chocolate for Ned and me, Hannah?"

"It's already on the stove," the housekeeper said. "I figured the two of you would be home about now, frozen stiff."

Ned dropped a kiss on her cheek. "Thanks, Hannah. You're a woman after my own hungry heart. While you're pouring the hot chocolate, why don't I microwave some popcorn?"

Hannah led the way into the kitchen, and Nancy headed for the living room. She sank down onto the sofa, picked up the phone, and punched in Angela's number.

Her friend answered immediately. "Nancy?

Oh, I'm so glad it's you! I was beginning to think you were never going to call me back."

"Ned and I were skating. We just got in, and Hannah gave me your message," Nancy said. "What's up?"

"Listen, I know I asked you and Ned to come to Long Island on the twenty-second, but— well, I've started working on your dress. I've cut it out and basted it together, and I think it's really going to be beautiful, but I'd like to fit it on you before I sew it on the machine, so I was wondering . . ." Angela's voice trailed off.

"Wondering what?" Nancy prompted.

"Well, I know this is a terrible imposition, and the two of you probably have lots of things to do in the next couple of weeks, so if you can't make it, I'll understand. . . ."

"I won't know whether we can make it or not until you tell me what *it* is," Nancy pointed out.

Angela giggled nervously. "I guess that would help, wouldn't it? Sorry. I'm so stressed out lately that sometimes I don't make much sense." Nancy heard her take a deep breath. "What I'm trying to say is, do you think you and Ned could come a little earlier?"

"I don't see why not," Nancy said. "Ned has exams next week, but winter break begins at Emerson right after that. When do you want us to come?"

"As soon as possible," Angela said. "When will Ned be finished with his exams?"

"The last one's Thursday morning—I think that's the nineteenth."

"Not until then? Oh, wow!" Angela sounded distressed. "Well, could you come that afternoon? Howard's plane can collect you at any time. Please say you will, Nancy. I really need you both!"

Startled by the urgency in her tone, Nancy replied, "I'll have to check with Ned, but I'm sure it will be okay. What's the rush, anyway? You sound kind of strange. Is anything wrong?"

"Oh, no! Like I said before, I just want to make sure your dress is absolutely perfect, that's all. Mother seems to be feeling a little better, and I'm marrying the most wonderful guy in the world. What could possibly be wrong?"

Nancy wasn't convinced. "That's what I want to know," she said, frowning. "We've been friends a long time, and it doesn't take a detective to figure out that you're not being honest with me. Come on, Angela—what's up?"

There was a long pause on the other end of the line. Finally Angela confessed, "You're right. Something *is* wrong, but I'd rather not talk about it over the phone."

"You and Rafe haven't had an argument or anything, have you?" Nancy asked.

"No, of course not," Angela said quickly. "It's just that something weird happened yesterday, and I'm hoping you'll be able to help me figure out what to do about it."

"What do you mean, weird? Can't you at least give me a clue?" Nancy urged.

"I'll tell you the whole story as soon as you get here," Angela said. "I'll ask Howard to have the plane waiting for you and Ned at O'Hare on the afternoon of the nineteenth. If you board by six o'clock, you ought to arrive on Long Island around eight-thirty. Our chauffeur will meet you at the airport and bring you to Soundview. Rafe's coming to dinner, and Howard has promised that he'll be here, too, for a change— he's been spending so much time at the office lately that he's hardly ever home. Mother says she's beginning to forget what he looks like. I can't wait for you to meet him."

"I'm looking forward to it, and so is Ned," Nancy said. "In the meantime, can't you talk to Rafe about whatever it is that's bothering you?"

"No, because I don't want to worry him."

"Well, you sure are worrying *me*," Nancy grumbled.

Angela sighed. "I'm sorry. I guess I shouldn't have mentioned it until you and Ned got here. And who knows? Maybe I'm overreacting. Forget it for now, okay? Gotta run."

Thoroughly mystified, Nancy hung up the

phone just as Ned came into the living room, carrying a tray with two mugs of steaming cocoa and a bowl of popcorn.

"So what's with Angela?" he asked, putting the tray down on the coffee table in front of the sofa. "Prewedding jitters?"

"Maybe. It sounds more serious than that, though. She's pretty upset about something, but she won't tell me what it is until she sees me." Nancy reached out, took a handful of popcorn, and began to munch absently. "Angela wants us to fly out on the afternoon of the nineteenth instead of the twenty-second. Is that okay with you?"

Dropping down beside Nancy, Ned put an arm around her. "Sure. My exams will be over, and I can't think of anything I'd rather do than spend more time with you, Nan. We've hardly seen each other lately."

"I know." Nancy snuggled into his embrace and rested her head on his shoulder. "I can't remember the last time we spent a day together like this. I've missed you, Ned, I really have."

"I've missed you, too." He pressed his lips to hers. "Mmmm! You taste delicious."

Nancy laughed. "That's the popcorn, silly! Better have some before it gets cold."

"I'll take my chances," he murmured, and kissed her again.

Ordinarily Ned's kisses thrilled Nancy right

down to her toes, but that night her response wasn't nearly as enthusiastic as usual, and Ned noticed.

"What's the matter, Nan?" he asked as she pulled away, a puzzled expression on his face. "Not in the mood for romance? Or am I losing my touch?"

Nancy shook her head. "None of the above." She picked up the mugs of cocoa and handed one to him, keeping the other for herself.

"Then what is it?"

"Angela," she said. "I'm really worried about her, Ned. She sounded—I don't know—almost desperate on the phone. She practically begged us to come early. I finally got her to admit that something was wrong, but when I tried to find out what it was, she said she wanted to wait until we got there, to tell us in person."

Ned shrugged. "Maybe she and Rafe are having problems. Angela's so nuts about the guy that she'd probably freak out over some minor disagreement."

"I don't think so," Nancy said. "I asked her if they'd had an argument, and she said no."

"Then it's probably prewedding jitters, as I said before," Ned stated. "And you have to admit that Angela's always had a tendency to make—"

"Mountains out of molehills." Nancy finished his sentence for him. "She's said the same thing herself many times."

"There you go. That proves my point." He put down his mug and reached out to massage her shoulders. "Take it easy, Nan. You're a dynamite detective, but we're not talking about one of your cases here, and Angela isn't one of your clients. This wedding is supposed to be a happy occasion, remember? I don't know about you, but I intend to enjoy every minute of it, beginning on Thursday when we wallow in the luxury of Mr. Tremain's private jet."

Nancy relaxed a little as Ned gently kneaded her tense muscles. She tried to convince herself that he was right about Angela. But her detective instincts told her that something was wrong: She had a terrible feeling that their friend was in real trouble.

Chapter

Three

NANCY LEANED FORWARD to peer through the window of the sleek black limousine as it purred along the narrow, winding road that led to the Chamberlain estate. It was past eight-thirty, and a rising moon gave the snowy landscape an unearthly glow, making it almost as light as day.

"Everything looks so beautiful, and so different from the first time I came here with my dad," Nancy said to Ned.

"Everything *is* different," Ned reminded her. "A lot has changed since then."

"That's for sure!" Nancy agreed. "Whoever would have guessed that three years later Angela's father would be dead, Mrs. Chamberlain remarried to his business partner, and Angela about to be married herself?"

"At least one thing hasn't changed—you and me. I'm glad we'll be spending Christmas together," Ned said, giving her hand an affectionate squeeze.

Nancy leaned back against the leather seat and moved closer to him. "Me, too." Then she sighed. "I only hope nothing happens to spoil it."

Ned frowned. "You're not still worrying about Angela, are you?"

"I'm trying not to, but I can't seem to help it," Nancy admitted.

"Well, try harder. That's an order," Ned joked. Then, glancing out the window, he added, "Hey, we're here!"

The limousine had passed between the imposing gateposts that flanked the entrance to Soundview's circular drive, and now it glided to a stop in front of the huge Tudor-style mansion. The chauffeur opened the limousine door for Nancy and Ned. As they got out, the door to the house swung open, and a slim, dark-haired girl in an ankle-length brown velvet dress raced down the steps to greet them.

"I thought you'd never get here. Oh, I'm so glad to see you both!" Angela cried. She flung her arms around Nancy, then turned to Ned, who gave her a bear hug.

"It's great to see you, too!" He lifted her off

the ground and spun her around in circles before setting her back on her feet.

Angela took her guests' hands and pulled them toward the house. "Come on inside before we all freeze." The chauffeur followed them with Nancy and Ned's luggage. "Arthur, would you please take the bags upstairs?" she asked. "Nancy will be in the room next to mine. Ned's room is directly across the hall."

"The red suitcase is mine," Nancy added.

As Arthur took the luggage upstairs, Parker, the tall, stately butler, approached and unbent enough to greet Nancy and Ned with a warm smile. "Good to see you again, Miss Drew and Mr. Nickerson," he said.

After he helped them off with their coats, Angela, chattering a mile a minute, led the way across the marble floor of the spacious entrance hall.

"Everyone is in the library. It's the coziest place to be on a day like today. I hope you had a good flight. I heard on the news that there was a big snowstorm starting in the Midwest, and I was afraid the plane might be grounded, but obviously it wasn't since you're here. . . ."

As she babbled on, Nancy got a good look at her friend for the first time, and what she saw disturbed her. Angela certainly wasn't the picture of a happy, blushing bride-to-be.

Although she was smiling brightly, her smile seemed forced. Her heart-shaped face was very pale, and there were dark circles under her green eyes, as though she hadn't been sleeping well.

Nancy wished she could speak to Angela in private and find out what the trouble was, but there was no time for that now. They were entering the library, and a ruggedly handsome, silver-haired man in an impeccably tailored gray business suit walked over to Ned and vigorously shook his hand.

"You're Ned Nickerson, of course," he said in a deep, booming voice. "It's a pleasure to meet you at last. I'm Howard Tremain, Angela's stepfather. Welcome to Soundview."

"Nice to meet you, too, sir," Ned replied with a smile.

As Ned crossed the room to where Felicia Tremain was seated by the fireplace in a wing chair, Howard turned toward Nancy.

"And this is the famous detective, Nancy Drew!" Nancy was surprised when instead of shaking her hand, he kissed her cheek. "I hope you don't mind, Nancy, I've heard so much about you from Angela and my wife that I feel as if I already know you."

Before Nancy could reply, Felicia Tremain called, "Stop monopolizing Nancy, Howard. I haven't seen her in ages. I want to welcome her, too, and introduce her and Ned to our future son-in-law."

"Of course you do, darling," her husband said. He took Nancy's arm and escorted her to Felicia's side.

Bending down to give Angela's mother a kiss, Nancy was shocked by the change in her since the last time they had met. In her youth Felicia had been a fashion model, beautiful and extremely thin, but the multicolored silk caftan she wore couldn't conceal the fact that she was now positively gaunt. Carefully applied makeup only emphasized her prominent cheekbones and sunken eyes, green like her daughter's but feverishly brilliant. Her jeweled necklace hung slackly about her throat.

"Nancy, how wonderful to see you, and how lovely you look!" Mrs. Tremain exclaimed. "I'm dying to hear all about your exciting career and Carson's latest case. But first you must both meet Rafe. Rafe, come say hello to Angela's friends."

Nancy looked over at the attractive, ponytailed young man in faded jeans and a baggy sweater who was standing in front of the fireplace with his arm around Angela's waist. The firelight flickered on a gold earring in his left ear.

Releasing Angela, Rafe strode forward and

shook hands with them both. "Hi, Nancy, Ned. Nice to meet you at last. From what Angie tells me, you're the only ones who made life bearable in River Heights."

His grin was infectious, and even though Nancy was concerned about Angela and shaken by her mother's appearance, she smiled back. "Oh, River Heights isn't all that bad. I've lived there my whole life, and I've managed to survive."

"I guess New York is definitely where it's at for a fashion designer like Angela," Ned said. "For an artist, too."

"New York's terrific, but Europe's even better." Rafe reached for Angela's hand and drew her close. "I still can hardly believe that Howard and Felicia are giving us a year in France and Italy for a wedding present. It's a dream come true for us."

"Well, I was thinking about a toaster, but Felicia talked me out of it." Mr. Tremain glanced at his wife and winked.

"Seriously," he continued, looking at Nancy and Ned, "Angela is very special to me—the daughter I always wanted but never had. Nothing could make her mother or me happier than helping these two make a wonderful start together."

"I'm sure Angela has told you how immensely talented Rafe is," Mrs. Tremain said to

Nancy and Ned. "He recently had a one-man show at the Silver Palette in Port Wellington that was very well received. Howard has commissioned him to do my portrait after he and Angela return from Europe." She made a face. "By then I hope I'll look a little less like the Wicked Witch of the West."

"Nonsense!" Mr. Tremain said sharply. "You're as beautiful as you ever were."

Just then Parker came into the library to announce that dinner was served. Mr. Tremain helped his wife rise from her chair, and arm in arm they led the procession to the dining room. When everyone was seated around the candlelit table, Howard excused himself.

"Felicia is on a restricted diet," he explained. "I always check with our cook to make sure her food has been properly prepared."

He returned a few minutes later, and Parker and a maid served the delicious meal. As Nancy savored her Cornish game hen à l'orange, her gaze flickered from Angela to her mother. Angela said very little and ate almost nothing; Mrs. Tremain talked nonstop, taking a few bites every now and then.

"So, Nancy, how is my dear friend Carson Drew?" she inquired. "I've been following his current case in the newspapers."

"Oh, he's great. The Steinbeck trial has

turned him into a bit of a stranger, though—I've hardly seen him since October," Nancy said with a sigh.

"Being a criminal attorney has to be a difficult job," Mrs. Tremain said. "Imagine how hard it would be, each time you take on a client, when you must look him in the eye and believe him when he tells you he's innocent."

"Mr. Drew once told me it's just as difficult to defend an innocent person as a guilty one," Ned noted. "That's always bothered me. I mean, you'd think innocence would count for something."

Everyone laughed. "Well, I'm sure Carson Drew is an impeccable judge of character. It's probably an important part of why he's so good at what he does," Mr. Tremain offered.

"Nancy's a pretty good judge of character, too," Angela said quietly. "It's something I've always appreciated about her."

"Well, thanks Angie, I—" Nancy stopped talking when she saw Mrs. Tremain grimace and drop her fork onto her plate with a small clatter.

"What's wrong, darling?" her husband asked anxiously.

"I—I don't feel very well," Mrs. Tremain murmured. "I hate to spoil this lovely party, but I'm afraid I must go to my room."

Her husband hurried to her side and helped her to her feet. "You did take your medicine today, didn't you?"

"Yes, she did," Angela said. "I gave it to her myself. Mother, do you want me to come with you?"

Clinging to her husband's arm, Felicia Tremain shook her head and managed a wan smile. "No, dear. Howard will take care of me while you entertain our guests. I'll see you all in the morning. I'm sure I'll be fine after a good night's rest."

As the older couple left the dining room, Rafe took Angela's hand. "Try not to worry, Angie," he said softly. "She always recovers from these attacks, you know that."

"Yes, I know, but that doesn't make them any easier to take," she murmured.

Dessert was served, and delicious though the pear tart was, Nancy noticed that no one finished theirs, not even Ned. With his help, Nancy tried to keep the conversation going, but it was difficult because neither Angela nor Rafe had much to say.

After coffee in the library, Rafe told them he had to leave. "I just got a part-time job with a contractor in the village, so I have to get up real early," he said. "It's lousy work, but at least it pays the rent," he said. He kissed Angela lightly on the cheek. "I'll come over tomorrow night

30

after work, Angie. And please get some sleep, okay? You look exhausted."

As soon as he was gone, Angela collapsed on the big leather sofa and buried her face in her hands.

Nancy and Ned sat down on either side of her, and Nancy gave her a hug. "Oh, Angela, I know how upset you must be about your mother, but——"

Angela raised her head. "It's not just Mother, although that's bad enough. I feel as if I'm having a nightmare, and I can't wake up! I told you on the phone that something weird had happened, remember?"

"I certainly do," Nancy said. "It's been driving me crazy ever since! You said you'd tell me about it when you saw me. Well, I'm here, and so is Ned. Will you please tell us now?"

Instead of answering, Angela jumped up and ran to a credenza on the other side of the room. She opened one of the doors and took out a white box, which she placed on the coffee table in front of the sofa.

"What's this?" Ned asked. "Looks like a wedding present."

"I suppose you could call it that," Angela said with a shiver. "It was delivered the day before I phoned you, Nancy. Open it."

As Nancy lifted the lid, she read aloud the words printed on it in flowing, metallic script:

"The Silver Palette. Isn't that the name of the gallery where Rafe had his one-man show?"

Angela nodded. "It's also an elegant gift shop. A lot of our wedding presents have come from there."

Setting the lid aside, Nancy parted the layers of tissue paper. "What on earth . . . ?" she exclaimed, staring at the shattered china inside.

Ned peered over her shoulder. "I don't know what that thing used to be, but whatever it was, it looks as though somebody deliberately smashed it to bits."

"It sure does," Nancy agreed. "What's this?" She took out a newspaper clipping from under the shards of china—and gasped. It was an announcement of Angela Chamberlain's engagement to Raphael Marino, and Angela's photograph had been viciously scribbled over with red marker.

"The announcement appeared in the local paper back in September," Angela said, her voice quivering. "Whoever sent it must have been holding on to it for months. And it gets worse." She took an envelope out of the pocket of her dress and gave it to Nancy with a trembling hand. "This just arrived in the mail today."

Nancy noted that the envelope bore a Port Wellington postmark—the town where Angela lived. Her name and address were printed on the envelope in neat block capitals, and so was the brief note inside.

" 'Miss Moneybags,' " Nancy read aloud. " 'That is what I call you because that is all you are. Rafe Marino doesn't care about you. He's only marrying you for your money. You might as well know that he is in love with someone else. Watch your step or you could be badly hurt.' "

There was no signature.

"Oh, wow!" Ned whispered. "No wonder you're a wreck."

"The worst part of it is that I'm afraid it's true." Angela's eyes filled with tears. "I never could figure out what Rafe saw in me. I mean, he could have anyone he wants. All the girls at school were after him. How he even managed to notice I was alive, I don't know, even now. You know me—I've hardly ever lifted my head up from my sewing machine long enough for anyone to notice me."

"Ange, has it ever occurred to you that Rafe found a kindred spirit when he met you? You're both kind, sensitive, talented artists. And you're both smart enough to have found each other, two wonderful needles in a haystack," Nancy insisted.

"Smart or just lucky?" Angela murmured.

"Who cares which it is?" Nancy placed her hands firmly on Angela's shoulders. "You are beautiful and talented. And best of all, you're one of a kind—real haute couture—not some off-the-rack design."

Angela chuckled in spite of herself.

"Furthermore," Nancy continued, "you're as worthy of Rafe's love as he is of yours. You need to trust yourself and Rafe. He's in love with you, and you're in love with him. It seems to me that's simple mathematics."

Nancy stood up as if the subject was closed. "Now, listen. I'll bet the person who wrote this note is the same one who sent the china, and that person obviously has a stupid grudge against you for some reason."

"Or for no reason at all," Ned put in. "There are a lot of weirdos out there, Angela. It's probably just some crackpot who gets a kick out of playing nasty practical jokes on the rich folks at Soundview."

"Do you really think that's all it is?" she asked.

"Yep," Ned said. "If you want my advice—and even if you don't—I'd say burn that stupid letter and the clipping, toss the china into the garbage where it belongs, and get on with your life."

Angela managed a faint smile. "Sounds like a plan to me. Thanks, Ned."

Before she could remove the gift box, the clipping, and the note, Nancy said quickly, "I'll take care of these. Why don't you go to bed now, Angela? Rafe was right—you look worn out."

"I guess I will," Angela said. "But I'd better check on my mother first. Sleep well, you two. See you in the morning."

When the door closed behind Angela, Nancy turned to Ned. "Sorry, but although Angela seems to buy your practical joke theory, I'm afraid I don't," she said quietly. "I think Angela has a very real enemy out there," she said, gesturing toward the window. "And I'm worried."

Chapter

Four

NANCY HAD TROUBLE getting to sleep that night, and when she finally dozed off, she dreamed of shadowy, threatening figures that pursued Angela through a dark and frightening landscape.

When she came downstairs the next morning, she found everyone else already seated around the table in the sun-filled breakfast room. Angela and Ned were wearing bulky sweaters and jeans, but Howard was dressed for the office in a three-piece suit. Felicia, wrapped in a soft pale-blue cashmere robe, seemed greatly improved.

"Sorry I'm late," Nancy said, sitting in the chair next to Ned.

He looked up from the stack of pancakes on his plate and grinned at her. "Morning, sleepyhead. I was kind of hoping you'd miss breakfast altogether so I could have all the flapjacks for myself."

"Don't worry, Ned," Angela said. "You won't starve—Beatrice made enough for an army." Angela turned to Nancy. "You'll also find sausage, blueberry muffins, and eggs on the buffet. Please help yourself."

Nancy was relieved to see that Angela looked and sounded more like her old self. The circles under her eyes were less pronounced, and there was even a little color in her cheeks.

Nancy served herself a blueberry muffin and scrambled eggs, and Felicia poured her a cup of coffee from the silver pot.

"I hope you slept well, Nancy," she said. "I certainly did. I feel so much better this morning!"

Mr. Tremain patted his wife's hand. "That's wonderful, darling. But you mustn't overdo. Remember what Dr. Harvey said."

"I know. Rest, rest, and more rest." Mrs. Tremain sighed. "And I *will* rest. The only thing I insist on doing today is getting a look at Nancy in that gorgeous red velvet gown Angela's making."

"You will," Angela promised. "I'm going to fit it on her later this morning."

"While you're doing that, I think I'll take a

walk," Ned said. "Unless you're making a matching velvet tux for me, that is."

Angela giggled. "You know, I never thought of that. But now that you mention it, it's not a bad idea."

"What are your plans for the rest of the day?" Mr. Tremain asked. Before Angela could reply, he suggested, "Why don't you take Nancy and Ned horseback riding? The fresh air and exercise will do you good. You've hardly left the house all week. It shouldn't be too cold. According to the weather report, the temperature will be in the high forties."

"Believe it or not, Howard has bullied Angela into taking riding lessons," Mrs. Tremain told Nancy and Ned.

"Now, just a minute, sweetheart," Mr. Tremain objected good-naturedly. "I wouldn't call it bullying. I simply encouraged Angela to take up some healthy outdoor activity to balance all the time she spends hunched over her drawing board in that studio of hers."

"And you were absolutely right," Felicia Tremain said quickly. "It's done her a world of good. Angela's become quite the horsewoman."

Mr. Tremain smiled. "It's true. She even won two ribbons in hunter competition at the North Shore Horse Show last summer," he said proudly. "You'll be amazed when you see her take her mare over the fences in the riding ring."

"Sounds like fun. I could use some exercise, too," Nancy said, and Ned agreed.

"Then that's what we'll do. But *after* the fitting," Angela said. "First things first."

"You must model your wedding gown for Nancy as well, dear," Mrs. Tremain said. "Wait till you see Angela in it, Nancy. She looks so beautiful, like a princess."

"Oh, Mother, *please!* You're embarrassing me," Angela protested, blushing. "It's not finished yet, and anyway, it's the dress that's beautiful, not me."

"Let's not hear any more of that," Mr. Tremain said. "You're a lovely, talented young woman, and don't you forget it." He glanced at his watch and stood up. "Well, I'm afraid I have to get going. I'll see you all this evening."

After they had finished their leisurely breakfast, Ned went for his walk while Angela took her mother and Nancy to a big, sunlit room on the third floor. It had once been used as a nursery for the original owners' children, but Angela had converted it into her design studio and workshop. Her drawing table was set up by the big bay window. Swatches of fabric, fashion sketches, and awards Angela had won at the institute covered the walls. A sewing machine stood in one corner, and dress forms held garments in various stages of completion, including Angela's wedding gown and Nancy's bridesmaid dress.

Here in her studio, surrounded by the tools of her trade, Angela blossomed. No longer shy and self-effacing, she immediately took charge. After she had settled her mother in a comfortable chair, she helped Nancy put on the red velvet gown.

"It fits you perfectly!" Mrs. Tremain exclaimed in delight, but Angela's eye was far more critical.

"Not quite. I'll have to make a few minor adjustments to the neckline and nip in the waist a little before I set in the zipper," she said. "Nancy's slimmer than I remembered."

Nancy laughed. "Thanks for those kind words!"

For the rest of the morning, Angela tucked, ripped, and basted until she was satisfied with the result. After lunch, Felicia took a nap while Nancy, Ned, and Angela changed into riding clothes.

"I'm sure Ned's right about that awful 'wedding present' and the note," Angela said as the three friends walked to the stables. "I never should have taken the whole thing so seriously." Her anxiety of the previous night seemed to have melted away like the light dusting of snow that was turning to slush under their booted feet.

Nancy didn't want to distress her, so she kept her doubts to herself. But she couldn't get the last sentence of the note out of her mind: "Watch your step or you could be badly hurt."

Well, Angela's safe now, she thought. Nothing can happen to her while she's with Ned and me, and until the wedding, I intend to make sure that one of us is never very far away.

Angela had phoned the stable before leaving the house to tell Norris, the head groom, that they were on their way. Starlight, her gray mare, Ranger, a chestnut gelding, and Donovan, a sturdy bay, were waiting for them when they arrived. A stable boy gave Angela a leg up, Nancy swung into Ranger's saddle, Ned mounted Donovan, and they trotted out of the stable yard.

Since the horses hadn't been out in more than a week, they were frisky, so Angela, Nancy, and Ned rode around the estate for a while to give the mounts a chance to settle down before tackling the jumps.

"You look great on a horse, Angie," Nancy called out to her friend. "Do you feel as good as you look?"

Angela grinned. "Well, I'm not sure I look so great, but I do love to ride. You can imagine how surprised I was to find that out, after all these years of avoiding any activity that didn't involve a bolt of fabric. I'll always be grateful to Howard for getting me into riding."

"Riding does have a nice way of clearing your head," Ned said. "I only wish I had the chance to do it more often."

"Oh, *that* explains why you look so rusty, cowboy," Nancy joked as she rode past Ned.

After a tour of the bridle paths that wound through Soundview's vast grounds, Angela led the way to the shore so they could take a brisk gallop along the beach. About a mile from Rocky Point, where a decrepit, abandoned pier jutted out into Long Island Sound, the shore became too rocky for the horses, so they doubled back, heading for the riding ring.

"Okay, Angela. Your stepfather said we'd be amazed by how well you jump, so amaze us," Ned teased.

Angela laughed. "Those ribbons Howard was boasting about were for fourth and sixth place, and there were only four riders in one class and six in the other!" she said with a laugh. "Why don't you each go around once, and then Starlight and I will give it a shot."

"All right. I'll go first," Nancy offered. Gathering up the big chestnut's reins, she urged him into a trot, then a canter. Ranger took the first jump without breaking stride and soared effortlessly over the other three with room to spare.

"Good boy!" Nancy patted the horse's sleek shoulder as they rode over to the others. "Your turn, Ned."

"Well, here goes nothing!" He nudged Donovan's sides with his heels, and the bay gelding lunged forward at breakneck speed, hooves pounding on the spongy ground. "Hey, wait for me!" Ned yelled. "This is supposed to be a team effort!"

In spite of his clowning, Ned was in complete control, and horse and rider sailed over jump after jump without a fault.

Now it was Angela's turn. Watching as she took Starlight around the course, Nancy was impressed by her friend's skill. So was Ned. "I *am* amazed," he confessed. "For somebody whose idea of exercise used to be waving around a pair of scissors and draping fabric, Angela sure has made progress."

The mare had jumped the first three hurdles with ease and was now approaching the last and highest one at a canter. But as Starlight sprang over the double-barred gate, Nancy saw to her horror that the mare's girth had suddenly given way and was hanging loose. Angela lurched to one side, and a split second later she and the saddle crashed to the ground.

Nancy dismounted in a flash. "Take the horses!" she shouted to Ned as she raced across the ring. "I'll go to Angela!"

Nancy dropped to her knees beside her friend's motionless body and pressed her fingers to the base of Angela's throat. To her immense relief, she felt a faint, erratic pulse.

"Angela, it's Nancy," she said urgently. "Can you hear me?"

After what seemed like ages, Angela's eyelids flickered, then slowly raised. "Nancy . . . Yes, I hear you. I'm—I'm okay, I think. . . . Wind knocked out of me, that's all. . . ."

"Thank goodness you're wearing your hard hat," Nancy said. "Without it, you could have been killed." Angela made a feeble attempt to rise, but Nancy ordered, "Don't move. You may have broken something."

Nancy gently manipulated Angela's legs and arms. Everything seemed to be in working order, so she allowed her to sit up very slowly.

"Oh, wow," Angela murmured groggily. "That's never happened to me before. I told you I'm not as good a rider as Howard thinks I am. When I felt the saddle start to slip, I didn't know what to do. I was scared out of my wits!"

"No wonder," Ned said. He had joined them after catching Starlight and tethering all three horses to the split-rail fence around the riding ring. "In a situation like that, there's nothing you *can* do except hope you don't break your neck. It's kind of like having the brakes of your car fail when you're driving."

"You were doing great until Starlight's girth gave out. It was just a freak accident. Even an Olympic rider would have fallen," Nancy said. "How are you feeling now, Angela? Do you think you'll be able to walk?"

"If not, I can always carry you," Ned offered. "I bet you don't weigh nearly as much as Nancy's suitcase."

Angela smiled faintly. "I think I can make it, if you'll give me a hand."

As Ned helped Angela to her feet, Nancy said, "Why don't you two start back to the house? I'll catch up with you after I ride Ranger to the stable and send somebody back for Angela's saddle and the other horses."

The Italian-style jumping saddle was still lying where it had fallen, and now something about the girth caught Nancy's eye. "That's odd," she murmured, examining it more closely. "These straps don't seem to be badly worn. In fact, it almost looks as though—"

"As though what?" Angela asked.

Nancy hesitated, then said reluctantly, "As though they've been cut partway through. The girth probably would have held up if you hadn't taken Starlight over those jumps. Stress must have done the rest."

Angela turned white as a sheet. Without Ned's support, she would have crumpled to the ground. "Then it wasn't an accident after all," she whispered. "Nobody uses that saddle but me. This was no practical joke—someone *wanted* me to fall. I knew it. Someone hates me enough to want me dead!"

Chapter

Five

ANGELA MADE Nancy and Ned promise not to say anything to her mother about what had happened in the riding ring for fear it would only worsen her condition. Nancy planned to tell Mr. Tremain, however, as soon as he got home from his office in Manhattan.

When they returned to the house, Nancy helped Angela ease her aching body into a hot bubble bath, then persuaded her to rest in her room until it was time to get ready for dinner.

"Please don't leave me, Nancy," Angela begged, clutching her hand. "I don't feel safe anymore, not even in my own home!"

So Nancy sat beside her canopied bed, her thoughts churning while Angela finally drifted off into a restless doze. Nancy no longer had any doubts that her friend was in grave danger. But from whom, and why? Angela had spent most of the past three years at school in Manhattan, returning to Soundview only for vacations, and had had little contact with anyone in the area. . . .

Except Rafe, said a small, insistent voice in Nancy's mind.

She shook her head impatiently. Even if Rafe was the fortune-hunter George, Hannah, and the writer of the anonymous poison-pen letter made him out to be, he wouldn't gain anything if Angela died before they were married and she came into her inheritance. No, it had to be somebody else, and Nancy was determined to find out that person's identity.

At six o'clock that evening, Nancy, Ned, and a very tense and frightened Angela were waiting for Howard Tremain in the library. Angela's mother had sent word that she wasn't feeling well and would not be coming down for dinner. When Mr. Tremain strode into the room a few minutes later, Angela ran to meet him.

"Angela! Thank goodness you're all right!" he exclaimed, putting his arms around her. "I stopped by the stable to speak to Norris about last month's feed bill, and he told me you'd had an accident in the riding ring."

"Starlight's girth broke just as we were going over the last jump, and when her saddle slipped off, I fell," she said. "But it *wasn't* an accident, Howard. Nancy thinks the straps that fasten the girth to the saddle had been tampered with."

"That's right, Mr. Tremain," Nancy said. "I examined them very carefully, and I'm positive that it wasn't ordinary wear and tear that made them break."

"It's a miracle Angela wasn't killed," Ned added.

"Now, just a minute," Mr. Tremain said, holding up a hand as if to stop the conversation. "Let me see if I have this straight. You're suggesting that somebody deliberately weakened the girth of Angela's saddle, expecting that sooner or later she'd have a nasty fall, correct?"

Nancy nodded. "Do you know of anyone who might have a reason to harm her?"

"Harm her?" Mr. Tremain echoed, then gave an incredulous laugh. "Of course not! If anybody is to blame for Angela's accident, it's Norris. That saddle is quite old, and the girth probably should have been replaced long ago. I've instructed him to order a new girth first thing Monday morning. And I warned him that if he doesn't shape up, he'll be looking for another job." He smiled at his stepdaughter. "I hope that sets your mind at ease, Angela. Now, if you'll all excuse me, I'll go upstairs to check on Felicia before we sit down to dinner."

As Mr. Tremain left the room, Ned shook his head. "I never thought I'd say this, but it looks as if you were wrong, Nancy."

"For Angela's sake, I'd love to be," Nancy replied. "But I know what I saw, and I'm as sure as I've ever been about anything that those straps didn't break on their own. And don't forget the china and the letter."

Angela shivered. "I wish I could. You think they're all connected, don't you?"

"Yes, I do. I also think it's time you let Rafe in on what's been happening," Nancy told her. "You've kept him in the dark long enough."

"*Too* long, if you ask me," Ned put in. "Rafe's your fiancé. If he doesn't deserve to know, who does?"

"You're right," Angela said. "I'll tell him everything when he comes over tonight."

Rafe arrived shortly after dinner. Howard Tremain greeted him, then went upstairs to spend the rest of the evening with his wife. As soon as the four young people were alone in the library, Angela sat down on the sofa next to Rafe. Holding his hand tightly, she told him the whole story.

Rafe listened in stunned silence. Even when Angela had finished, he didn't say a single word. He seemed to be in a state of shock.

Nancy had been watching him intently, and now she decided to play a hunch. "You know something about all this, don't you, Rafe?" she asked.

"No!" he exclaimed. "That is, I don't *know* anything—"

Nancy pounced. "But you suspect something—or some*one,* right?"

Rafe hesitated, then said, "Okay, here goes. A girl I know in Port Wellington, Shannon Mulcahey, works at the Silver Palette, selling gifts and making deliveries. And I think her cousin Jeremy is a part-time stable hand here at Soundview."

"So you're suggesting that this girl could have delivered the package to Angela and also had access to the stables through her cousin?" Nancy asked.

Rafe nodded.

"But opportunity doesn't mean anything without motive," Nancy pointed out. "Does Shannon have a grudge against Angela for some reason?"

"How could she?" Angela asked with a puzzled frown. "I've never even met her, although I suppose I must have seen her in the gift shop or the gallery. What does she look like, Rafe?"

He shifted uncomfortably in his seat. "Dark hair, pretty, about your height and build . . ."

Angela's green eyes widened. "Oh, I know who you mean. So that's Shannon Mulcahey. *Pretty* isn't the word for her. She's *gorgeous!*"

"I don't get it," Ned said. "Nancy's right. Where's the motive? Why would a total stranger want to prevent Angela's marriage, much less try to murder her?"

Nancy had been putting two and two together, and she was pretty sure she knew the answer to that question. "Shannon may be a stranger to Angela, but not to Rafe. In fact, she's in love with you, isn't she?" she asked him.

Rafe stared at her. "How did you know that?"

"It's obvious," Nancy said. "Why else would you immediately suspect Shannon of trying to ruin your relationship with your fiancée?"

Rafe's shoulders slumped. "She keeps saying she's crazy about me, but sometimes I think she's just plain crazy. We dated for a while, but Shannon was a lot more serious about me than I was about her. She was jealous and possessive, always making melodramatic scenes if I so much as spoke to another girl. About a year ago I broke up with her, but Shannon hasn't been able to accept the fact that we're through and that I'm in love, *really* in love, with someone else. With you, Angie," he said softly, putting his arm around her.

"Shannon went ballistic when our engagement was announced—threatened to kill herself, threatened to kill me, the whole bit—but I didn't pay any attention because I'd heard it all before. Until you told me about what you've been going through, it never occurred to me that she might actually turn on you, Angie. Why didn't you tell me sooner?"

"Why didn't you tell *me* about Shannon?" Angela countered.

"I don't honestly know," he confessed. "I guess because I didn't think it was all that important."

"Maybe not to you, but it's very important to me." Angela's voice trembled. "And it's obviously even more important to Shannon! How do you think it makes me feel to know that you're still involved with a girl—a very *beautiful* girl—you used to date?"

"I'm not 'involved' with Shannon," Rafe protested. "Whatever there was between us was over long ago." He tried to pull Angela close, but she edged away.

"Is it really over, or"—Angela swallowed hard—"are you still in love with her?"

"No! You're not making sense, Angie. Believe me, you're the only girl I love!"

Angela leaped to her feet. "I don't know what to believe anymore!" she cried. "I was so thrilled when we first started going out, but I was afraid you were only interested in me because of my inheritance. When you told me that you loved me for myself, I wanted desperately to believe it, so I did. Maybe I shouldn't have. Maybe you're just marrying me for my money, like that awful letter said!"

Rafe stood up. "That really hurts, Angie," he said quietly, controlling his anger with great effort. "I thought we had something very special between us. I guess I was wrong. If you think I'm some kind of fortune hunter who'd fool around with another girl behind your back, then we have nothing more to say to each other!"

With that, he stormed out. Seconds later the front door slammed behind him, and Angela ran from the room in tears.

Stunned, Ned and Nancy stared at each other. Finally Nancy said, "First thing tomorrow morning I intend to go to the Silver Palette and check out Shannon Mulcahey." She stood and moved toward the door. "But right now I'd better see if Angela's okay."

"You don't think Rafe is involved with Shannon, do you, Nan?" Ned asked.

Nancy paused at the door. "It seems unlikely, since he was the one who brought her up," she said. "Still, I guess it's possible. Rafe certainly seemed sincere, but for all we know, he could have been putting on an act. And if that's the case, Angela is in for a miserable marriage—if she lives to see her wedding day!"

Chapter

Six

HOWARD TREMAIN HAD put one of Sound-view's cars at Nancy and Ned's disposal for their visit, and when they came outside at nine o'clock on Saturday morning, a sleek red Corvette was parked on the circular drive.

Ned whistled in admiration. "Decent wheels!"

"Not too shabby," Nancy agreed.

Ned took her in his arms, and their lips met in a long, sweet kiss. When they parted, he said, "Do you realize that's the first time we've kissed since we got here?"

Nancy sighed. "We have a lot of catching up to do."

"Better believe it! Take care, Nan," Ned said as she slid behind the wheel. "Don't worry about Angela. I won't let her out of my sight."

He had volunteered to stay at the estate to keep an eye on Angela and to prevent any further "accidents" while Nancy drove to the village in search of Shannon. "Any idea when you'll be back?"

"Hard to tell," Nancy said, buckling her seat belt. "Probably around midafternoon. I'll have to give myself time to get ready for the Freemans' dinner dance at the country club in honor of Angela and Rafe. It starts early, so Mrs. Tremain will be able to come, if only for a short while."

Ned slapped his forehead. "Oh, brother! I'd forgotten all about it. Since the bride and groom just had a major fight, that's bound to be loads of fun. I wonder if Rafe will even show up."

"He can't very well back out now, and neither can Angela, although she told me last night she wished she could," Nancy told him. "Mr. Freeman was a good friend of her father, and Mrs. Freeman is still very close to Angela's mother." She turned the key in the ignition, and as the powerful engine roared to life, she said, "Well, I'm off. Wish me luck."

"I always do," Ned said sincerely. "Happy hunting!"

The sky was overcast, and a light snow was falling when Nancy pulled into a parking place on Port Wellington's Main Street. Although wreaths hung from every lamppost and the windows of all the quaint little shops were filled with Christmas decorations, Nancy was definitely not in a holiday mood as she got out of the car and headed for the Silver Palette.

Bells tinkled merrily over the door, and the scent of spicy potpourri tickled Nancy's nose when she walked inside.

"Morning!" a cheerful voice rang out. A plump, middle-aged woman wearing a long, handmade beaded necklace and a loose garment made of hand-loomed fabric bustled up to her. "Seems like we're going to have a white Christmas, doesn't it? I'm Chloe. Can I help you?"

"I hope so," Nancy replied. "I'm looking for Shannon Mulcahey."

"Sorry, dear," the plump woman said. "I'm afraid you're out of luck. Shannon's not here on weekends. Are you a friend of hers?"

"We have a mutual friend who asked me to look her up," Nancy said. "Could you tell me how I can get in touch with her?"

Before Chloe could answer, the bells tinkled again, and several people entered the shop. "Oh, good! *Real* customers!" she chirped. As she hurried off to wait on the new arrivals, she stuck her head into the gallery and called,

"Alison, would you please give Miss—" She turned to Nancy. "What did you say your name was, dear?"

"I didn't say, but it's Drew, Nancy Drew," Nancy replied.

A tall, thin girl dressed all in black with shaggy blond hair came out of the gallery, and the woman said, "Oh, Alison, there you are! Please give Miss Drew Shannon's address and phone number. She's a friend of hers."

Alison eyed Nancy coldly. "I didn't think Shannon had any friends—not female ones, anyway."

"Well, we're not really friends," Nancy said. "I'm not from around here, but we have a friend in common."

She followed Alison to the wrapping desk at the rear of the shop and waited while the other girl tore off a piece of paper from a notepad and scribbled something down. "Here you go," Alison said, handing the paper to Nancy. "I doubt if you'll be able to reach her, though. Shannon's probably spending the day with her boyfriend, Glenn."

Nancy didn't have to fake her surprise. "Glenn? Gee, that's news to me! The last I heard, she was nuts about some guy with a weird name—Raphael, or something like that."

"You mean Rafe Marino."

"That sounds right." Nancy tucked the piece of paper into her shoulder bag. "Whatever happened to him?"

"They broke up. Actually, *he* broke up with *her* right after he met this girl at the art school they both went to in the city," Alison said. "They got engaged back in September, and they're going to be married at Christmas. Rafe's fiancée is filthy rich, and what's more, she lives right outside Port Wellington at this big estate called Soundview. Ever heard of it?"

"As I said, I'm not from around here," Nancy replied, evading the question. She glanced at a stack of boxes wrapped in white with elaborate silver bows. "Wedding presents?"

Alison nodded. "I'll be taking them to Soundview later today. Shannon makes deliveries during the week, and I do it on weekends."

"Poor Shannon!" Nancy sighed in mock sympathy. "I'd sure hate to deliver wedding presents to my former boyfriend's fiancée. But since Shannon has a new boyfriend, I guess she's gotten over Rafe."

"Are you kidding? She's still nuts about him!" Alison scowled. "There's nothing she wouldn't do to get him back. The only reason Shannon started dating Glenn MacInnes was to make Rafe jealous. She's just using him—she doesn't really care about Glenn at all."

"But *you* do, don't you?" Nancy was beginning to get the picture, and it wasn't a pretty one.

Alison abruptly turned away. "Not that it's any of your business, but yes, I do," she muttered. "Glenn was my boyfriend until Shannon got her hooks into him. Now he's so crazy about her that I might as well not even exist."

"And you and Shannon still work together here at the Silver Palette? Wow, that must be rough," Nancy said. This time her sympathy was genuine.

"Rough?" Alison gave a short, bitter laugh. "That's putting it mildly. Try impossible! After Shannon stole Glenn, I asked Chloe to change my schedule. Now I come in on weekends and evenings when Shannon's off. I haven't laid eyes on that witch in months, and if I never see her again it'll be too soon."

The bells over the door had been tinkling nonstop, and now the shop was crowded with customers. "Alison!" Chloe yelled. "Get a move on! I could use a little help here!"

"Coming!" Alison yelled back. "Got to get to work," she said to Nancy. "If you find your friend Shannon, do me a favor. Tell her I hope she has a rotten Christmas."

As Nancy edged her way around the growing throng of holiday shoppers and stepped outside, she shivered, but not because of the cold. According to Alison, Shannon was ruthless in her pursuit of Rafe and would stop at nothing to get him back—and that might very well include trying to murder Rafe's bride-to-be.

More determined than ever to track Shannon down, Nancy took the scrap of paper out of her shoulder bag and checked the address Alison had written down. Asking directions from a passerby, she found that 44 Cranford Street was within walking distance. She found it easily enough, but although Nancy rang the bell of the upstairs apartment in the small clapboard house several times, there was no response. At last she pressed the bottom bell, and the door opened immediately.

"You don't give up easy, do you?" said the sour-faced man in the doorway when Nancy asked for Shannon. "Shannon ain't here. Don't know where she's gone, don't know when she'll be back, don't want to be bothered." With that, he slammed the door in Nancy's face.

"Friendly type," Nancy muttered.

She trudged back to Main Street and spent the next several hours snooping around the village without turning up a trace of Shannon Mulcahey. Deciding to shift her focus to Glenn MacInnes, Nancy looked him up in the phone book and dialed his number, not really expecting him to be home. She was right. All she got was the message on his machine. During lunch at the Copper Kettle, however, Nancy did manage to find out where Glenn worked from a chatty waitress. She went to Philbin's Hardware that afternoon.

"I'm Glenn's cousin Bess Marvin from Chicago, and I need to speak to him right away," she told the bearded man behind the counter. "When I called him, he wasn't home. I realize it's Glenn's day off, but do you happen to know how I can get in touch with him? It's kind of important—family stuff, you know?"

The man scratched his head. "Well, now, I'd like to help you, Miss Marvin, but I don't have any idea where Glenn is today. He mentioned he was going somewhere with his girlfriend, but he didn't say where and I didn't ask. For all I know they might have gone away for the weekend."

Another dead end.

Nancy left the store and retraced her steps to the red Corvette, where she called Ned on the car phone to tell him she was on her way back to Soundview.

Nancy had a bad feeling in the pit of her stomach as she headed toward Soundview. Someone was trying to kill Angela—and Nancy's prime suspect was nowhere to be found.

Chapter
Seven

On Saturday night the ballroom of the Port Wellington Country Club was festooned with pine garlands twinkling with tiny white lights. An elaborately decorated Christmas tree sparkled in one corner, and on the bandstand a five-piece combo played pop classics while festively dressed couples danced. The tables surrounding the dance floor were draped in crimson damask, and candles nestling in Christmas centerpieces flickered on the smiling faces of the guests. It was the perfect setting for a joyous celebration of Angela and Rafe's upcoming marriage, Nancy thought, and under other conditions, she would have been having a wonderful time. As it was, however, she wasn't feeling at all cheery.

After wasting most of the day on a wild-goose

chase without catching so much as a glimpse of Shannon Mulcahey, Nancy had returned to Soundview to bathe and change for the dance. Promptly at six o'clock, Mr. and Mrs. Tremain drove off in their Mercedes, followed by Nancy, Ned, and a miserable Angela in the limousine.

According to Ned, Rafe had phoned earlier that day while Nancy was out, but he had refused to talk to his fiancée. Instead, he'd left a message with Parker that he would meet her at the club, and from the moment Rafe arrived, Nancy was uncomfortably aware of the tension between him and Angela.

"The only good thing about this evening is dancing with you," Ned murmured in Nancy's ear as they swayed in rhythm to a romantic melody. "It wasn't too bad while Mr. and Mrs. Tremain were here—at least Angela and Rafe put on a show for their benefit. But ever since they left, Angela's been about as lively as a zombie, and so has Rafe."

Nancy rolled her eyes. "Tell me about it! It's not easy pretending to the Freemans and their friends that nothing's wrong when the bride and groom are barely speaking and didn't even arrive in the same car."

"To tell you the truth, Rafe's attitude is beginning to bug me," Ned said. "Okay, he's ticked off at Angela, but it wouldn't have killed him to come with the rest of us instead of driving here himself."

He glanced at his watch and winced. "It feels like midnight, but it's not even ten o'clock."

"Why don't we see if the happy couple is ready to leave, okay?" Nancy suggested. "I heard Angela tell the chauffeur to pick us up at ten-thirty. If we're lucky, by the time we say goodbye to everybody, Arthur ought to be out in front."

Ned brightened. "Good thinking. Let's go."

They threaded their way through the crowd of dancers to the candlelit table where Angela and Rafe sat in glum silence, avoiding each other's eyes. They were every bit as eager to get away as Nancy and Ned were, and after thanking their hosts and retrieving their coats, all four of them headed for the exit.

But as they passed through the club's front door onto the main terrace, there was no sign of the limousine. They were about to go back inside until Arthur arrived when Rafe suddenly stopped dead in front of them.

"What are *you* doing here?" he asked harshly.

"Waiting for you, of course," a husky feminine voice purred from the shadows. "Everybody in town has heard about the Freemans' dinner dance, so I knew where to find you."

As the strikingly beautiful, dark-haired young woman stepped into the light shed by the ornate lanterns on either side of the entrance, Angela gasped.

So did Nancy. Gripping Ned's arm, she whispered, "That *has* to be Shannon Mulcahey!"

Rafe's hands were clenched tightly at his sides. "Shannon, I don't know what kind of game you're playing, but whatever it is, count me out," he said. "Just go away and leave us alone!"

" 'Us'?" Her blazing eyes darted from Rafe to Angela. "Oh, you mean you and little Miss Moneybags." She smiled when Angela flinched. "The name rings a bell, doesn't it? It's all true, you know, everything I wrote in that letter."

"Don't listen to her, Angie," Rafe pleaded. "She's just trying to mess with your head!"

But Angela didn't seem to hear him. She was staring at Shannon as though she were hypnotized.

Shannon paid no attention to him, either. "Unfortunately for both of us, Rafe couldn't resist the temptation to get his hands on your inheritance," she said. "But you have to understand that he'll always be in love with me. If you marry him, he'll break your heart to pieces just like that pretty china plate."

Angela finally found her voice. "You tried to kill me, too, didn't you?" she whispered. "You're the one who tampered with my saddle girth, hoping that I'd fall and break my neck."

Shannon gave an incredulous laugh. "What are you talking about? I don't even know what a saddle girth is. You are deluded, you poor little rich girl. I actually feel sorry for you. Take my advice and let Rafe go. You can always buy yourself another fiancé."

"Shut up!" Rafe shouted. He lunged at Shannon, but instead of trying to elude him, she threw her arms around his neck.

"Oh, Rafe, you know it's true. You *do* love me!" she cried. "We were meant to be together forever and ever. Tell her that! She'll believe it if she hears it from you!"

As Shannon clung to him, a pickup truck roared up the driveway and came to a screeching halt in front of the club. A brawny young man in a ski jacket and jeans leaped out, leaving the lights on and the motor running. His face was contorted with rage. He took the steps two at a time, shoved Shannon aside, grabbed Rafe by the shoulder, and spun him around.

Before he could land a punch on Rafe's jaw, Ned sprang into action. He tackled the stranger from behind, knocked him to the ground, and held him down with one knee firmly planted in the small of his back.

"Nice work." Nancy said.

"Get off me, you jerk!" Rafe's assailant yelled. He struggled to escape, but Ned kept him pinned to the terrace floor.

"Maybe I will and maybe I won't," he said. "It depends. Who are you, anyway?"

The guy scowled. "Who wants to know?"

"Who cares?" Shannon snapped irritably. "You got exactly what you deserved, Glenn MacInnes. You had no right to follow me here and attack Rafe like that!"

Well, surprise, surprise, Nancy thought. Alison's ex-boyfriend.

Ned cautiously released his hold on Glenn, and he stood up, brushing the snow off his jeans and glaring at Shannon.

"No *right?* Give me a break!" he shouted. "Who has a better right, I'd like to know? You say you want to go to Manhattan today to skate at Rockefeller Center, so I take you there. You want to see the Christmas show at Radio City Music Hall, so we go. Then you suddenly decide you don't want to spend the evening in the city like we planned, so I bring you home. And what do *you* do? You sneak out behind my back to keep a date with *him!*" He pointed at Rafe.

"Glenn, there's no date here, believe me," Rafe said. "I haven't spoken to Shannon in months. My fiancée, her friends, and I were getting ready to leave, and Shannon just turned up out of the blue. We broke up a long time ago—you know that!"

"I thought I did, but apparently Shannon hasn't gotten the message," Glenn said grimly.

69

He walked over to her and seized her wrist. "Come on. You've caused enough trouble for one night. We're getting out of here."

With one quick, sinuous movement Shannon twisted out of his grasp. "Don't touch me!" she screamed, backing away. "I'm not going anywhere with you, not now, not ever. As of this minute, we're through! You're a loser, Glenn, and you always will be. I'm sick of the sight of you, so get out of my life!"

Glenn stiffened as though he'd been slapped. The color drained from his ruddy face, and his voice shook with fury as he said, "Don't do this to me, Shannon, I'm warning you!"

She laughed. "Oh, I'm *so* scared! Hey, I've got a great idea. Why don't you go crawling to Alison? She's probably dumb enough to take you back. And here's an even better idea— maybe you can console poor little Miss Moneybags when Rafe dumps her. I guarantee you'll never get another crack at a fortune like hers."

Shannon ran down the steps to her car and got in. "I'll meet you at Rocky Point at midnight, Rafe," she called. "Don't keep me waiting!" She gunned the motor and sped down the driveway.

For a moment Glenn seemed frozen to the spot. Then he raced for his truck and took off after her. He never saw the limousine coming toward him from the opposite direction.

Angela screamed, but the limo swerved out of Glenn's way just in time to avoid a collision. It skidded on a patch of ice before the driver regained control and pulled to a stop in front of the club. Nancy couldn't see the chauffeur from where she stood, but a quick glance at the license plate told her it was Soundview's limousine.

Angela immediately started down the steps, but Rafe held her back. "Angie, don't go. We have to talk."

She turned to face him, unshed tears glinting in her eyes. "There's absolutely nothing to talk about. Shannon's meeting you at the Point, remember? You'd better not keep her waiting!"

Rafe grabbed her by the shoulders. "She can wait out there forever for all I care. Everything she said was a pack of lies. I told you, she's crazy," he said urgently. "I'm not in love with Shannon, and I'm not in love with Angela Chamberlain, the heiress, either. I'm in love with *you*, Angie. Believe me, Shannon will never come between us again—I promise."

Angela shook her head. In a flat, toneless voice she replied, "How can I believe in a promise you won't be able to keep? Please let go of me, Rafe. I want to go home."

His hands fell to his sides, and Angela got into the limousine, followed by Nancy and Ned. As the limo pulled away, Nancy looked out the rear window. Rafe was still standing on the terrace, a tortured expression on his handsome face.

Nancy turned back to Angela, who was huddled in a corner of the seat. She was hugging herself, and her eyes were closed. She looked so pale that Nancy was alarmed.

"Are you okay?" she asked.

"No. How could I be? It's all over," Angela said in that same listless monotone. "Rafe keeps saying Shannon's crazy, but I'm the crazy one for thinking he could really care about me." She opened her eyes and stared straight ahead. "Shannon fought for him, and now she's won. The wedding's off."

Chapter

Eight

ARE YOU SURE you want to do this, Angela? Call off the wedding, I mean," Ned said. "I don't blame you for being angry after what happened tonight, but maybe you ought to sleep on it and then talk things over with Rafe in the morning."

"I've already heard Rafe's side of the story, and so have you and Nancy," Angela said wearily. "What would be the point of listening to it all over again?"

Nancy frowned. "But what if he's telling the truth? Okay, Shannon Mulcahey's a very beautiful girl, and Rafe dated her before he met you. So what? Everyone has a history. That doesn't mean he's still involved with her, no matter what she says. Frankly, I wouldn't trust Shannon any farther than I could throw her. I'd take

Rafe's word over hers any day. If you really love him, at least give him the benefit of the doubt."

"Don't you see? It's the doubt I can't stand." Angela moaned. "Until two days ago I didn't know Shannon Mulcahey existed, and now she's all I can think about! I can't stop wondering about her and Rafe. The only thing I know for sure is that she hates me like poison. If I married Rafe, I'd never feel safe as long as Shannon's alive."

When the limousine arrived at Soundview a few minutes later, Angela asked Nancy and Ned to come with her for moral support while she broke the news to her stepfather. "I'll need Howard to help cushion the blow when I tell Mother tomorrow," she said. "She's very fond of Rafe, and I'm afraid she's going to be terribly upset."

They found Howard going over a stack of papers at his desk in the library. He looked up and smiled in greeting. "Well, now, I want to hear all about what went on after Felicia and I left," he said.

Then, seeing Angela's stricken expression, he stood and walked toward her. His smile faded. "What's wrong, Angela?"

The tears Angela had managed to hold back until then flowed down her cheeks. She sat down on the couch, and Nancy and Ned sat beside her, listening silently as she poured out an account of all that had happened over the last few weeks, from the delivery of the broken China to Shannon's appearance at the country club that night.

"So you see, Howard, it's impossible for me to go through with this wedding," Angela said, sighing wearily as she leaned her head back on the couch. "There's nothing to do but call it off. What kind of life could we have together after all that has happened? I love Rafe, but all the trust is gone."

Nancy had noticed Mr. Tremain's outrage growing with every painful word his stepdaughter spoke. He did not interrupt her, however. When she finally finished, he exclaimed, "This Shannon is obviously out of her mind! She belongs in an institution—and so does Rafe if he's still in love with her as you suspect." He turned to Nancy. "I owe you an apology. From what I've just heard, it seems that you were right and Angela's fall yesterday wasn't an accident after all."

Then he turned to Angela. "Please don't be afraid," Howard said softly. "I won't let anyone harm you." As her sobs began to subside, he went on, "Here's what we're going to do. Tomorrow morning I'll take you to the police station to swear out a complaint against Shannon Mulcahey. Then we'll work on getting an order of protection from the court. In the meantime, I want you to get some rest."

"Would you like me to sleep in your room with you tonight, Angela?" Nancy asked. "I'd be glad to."

Angela shook her head. "Thanks, but I really want to be alone. All of a sudden my whole life has fallen apart, and I don't know if I'll ever be able to pick up the pieces."

"Of course you will!" Howard said. "To begin with, you have your career. Anyone can see you're going to be a tremendously successful fashion designer."

"Funny—that used to be the only thing I ever dreamed of, but somehow it doesn't seem very important anymore," Angela said softly.

"Not now, maybe, but after all this is over, it will again. Go to bed, dear. I'll be working here for a while longer, so if you need me for anything, you know where to find me." Howard kissed her gently on the forehead. "Try not to worry. Everything's going to be all right."

Nancy couldn't shake her troubled thoughts as she got ready for bed that night. The events of the past three days played over and over in her mind like a continuous loop of videotape— the threatening letter, Angela's fall from her horse, her argument with Rafe, and finally the violent scene at the country club that had frightened Angela into breaking her engagement to the man she loved.

And beautiful, spiteful Shannon Mulcahey was responsible for it all.

Nancy's thoughts turned to Rafe. Whether he wanted to marry Angela for love or for money, Nancy wondered whether he'd give her up without a struggle. As long as Shannon considered Angela her rival, Angela would be in danger. Although Howard seemed confident that an order of protection would guarantee her safety, Nancy knew that no matter how alert the police were, they couldn't be everywhere at once. And no court order could keep Shannon away if she was determined to harm Angela.

Nancy paced back and forth, too worried about her friend even to think about going to bed. Around midnight she couldn't stand it any longer. Angela had said she wanted to be alone, but she knew that depressed people often said that when they didn't mean it. Nancy pulled on her robe, slipped out of her room, and knocked on Angela's door.

"It's me, Nancy," she called softly. "May I come in?"

There was no answer.

She knocked again. "Angela, are you okay?"

Still no answer.

Carefully Nancy turned the knob and opened the door.

The room was empty. Her heart pounding, Nancy checked the adjoining bathroom, but Angela wasn't there. The only trace of her was her evening gown lying on the floor beside the bed.

The sound of a car's engine drew Nancy to the window. Although thick clouds obscured the moon, the estate's grounds were well lit, and she could clearly see Angela's Porsche speeding away from the house. Where was she going, and why? In her present state of mind, Nancy thought, the last place Angela should be was behind the wheel of a car!

The keys to the red Corvette were still in Nancy's purse, but she knew that even if she took off after Angela without stopping to get dressed, she would never be able to overtake her. Then Nancy saw Mr. Tremain's Mercedes racing down the drive, and she heaved a sigh of relief. Thankful that he meant to stick close to his stepdaughter, she went back to her own room and climbed into bed.

Nancy hardly slept at all for the rest of that night. She tossed and turned as she waited anxiously for Angela and her stepfather to return, but by five o'clock there was still no sign of them. Unable to lie in bed a moment longer, Nancy got up and put on jeans, a heavy sweater, and boots. As she stepped into the hall, she saw

Ned coming out of his room. He was fully dressed, too.

"Couldn't sleep either, huh?" he said, giving her a kiss.

"Not a wink," Nancy said wearily. "Wait till you hear the latest. Angela's disappeared."

Ned stared at her. "You're kidding!"

"I wish I was. She drove off hours ago. Mr. Tremain went after her in his car, and they haven't come back yet."

"Well, if Angela's stepfather is with her, she's probably okay," Ned said. "He wouldn't let anything happen to her."

"Not if he could help it. But he might not have been able to catch up with her," Nancy pointed out. "Or what if they had an accident? There was a lot of ice on the roads tonight. They might both be dead."

"Take it easy, Nan," Ned soothed. "That's a pretty dire scenario. How about a more cheerful version? Try this one: Suppose Angela wants to be alone to do some thinking. She drives off and ends up at an all-night diner somewhere. Her stepfather follows her there, and at this very moment they're sipping coffee, having a heart-to-heart about the whole situation."

Nancy sighed. "You're right. We have no way of knowing what the real story is. I just hate feeling so helpless! I guess there's nothing we can do right now, though, except hang loose and wait."

Ned put his arm around her shoulders. "While we're hanging, let's get our jackets and go for a walk on the beach, okay? I think we could both use some fresh air and exercise to clear the cobwebs out of our brains. And who knows? When we get back, maybe Angela and Mr. Tremain will be here, wondering what's happened to *us!*"

The sun had not yet risen when Nancy and Ned came out of the house. After they left the lighted area of the estate, it seemed more like the middle of the night than early morning. As they walked along the shore, Ned put his arm around Nancy, and she slipped her arm around his waist.

"Doesn't it seem as if people always take the hard road in relationships?" Ned wondered aloud.

"I was just thinking the same thing," Nancy said. "In spite of how rich she is, Angela hasn't had an easy time of it, especially with her father dying and all. Wouldn't it be nice if there weren't all these characters—you know, Shannon, Glenn, and who knows who else—complicating what seemed to be such an easy, sweet romance between Angela and Rafe."

Ned squeezed Nancy's shoulders and

touched his head to hers. "You mean easy and sweet like ours?" he whispered.

Nancy hugged Ned tighter. "Yeah, sort of like that. You have to admit, though, it's not *always* easy between us. Sometimes we have to work at it."

"That's true, but no matter what, it seems we never lose our cool. It's one of the things I love best about you—I can always be sure you'll think the problem out and do the right and reasonable thing." Ned kissed Nancy's hair lightly.

"Let's hope we can keep up our good record," Nancy said with a little laugh.

A cold breeze blew off Long Island Sound, and Nancy shivered. "How about we jog for a while?" Nancy suggested. "That wind is really fierce."

Ned rubbed his gloved hands together. "Great idea," he said. "It's colder out here than I thought. I could use some warming up."

They jogged along the shore for a while, and then Ned challenged Nancy to a race.

"You're on," she said promptly. The sky was gradually turning from black to sullen gray, and looking down the beach toward the Point, Nancy could make out the dim outline of the abandoned pier. "Race you to those big rocks down by the pier!" she shouted. Although Ned's legs were longer, his boots were heavier than

Nancy's and slowed him down. She sprinted ahead, taking deep breaths of the cold, salty air and began to feel more like herself again. For the moment at least, Nancy was able to push all her worries to the back of her mind, focusing only on winning the race.

But as she approached the pier, she glimpsed something lying on the rocks below, something dark and shapeless. Nancy slowed down, straining her eyes to see what it was. And when she finally did, she stopped in her tracks, frozen with horror.

"What's the matter, Nan? Out of steam?" Ned teased as he caught up with her. "You'll never beat me that way."

Nancy didn't reply. She couldn't. She felt as though her heart had suddenly lodged in her throat. Without a word she pointed at what she had just spotted on the rocks ahead.

It was the crumpled body of a slender, dark-haired girl.

"Angela!" Ned gasped.

Chapter

Nine

"IT'S NOT ANGELA—it's Shannon!" Nancy shouted as she scrambled over the rocks to where Shannon lay sprawled with her arms outflung.

"Is she . . . ?" Ned couldn't bring himself to say the word.

Nancy finished the sentence for him. "Dead? I don't know, but I'm going to find out."

Shannon's eyes were closed, and her beautiful face was as gray as that of a corpse.

Nancy stripped off her gloves. Pressing her fingertips to the unconscious girl's throat below the jawline, she felt a faint, fluttering pulse.

"She's alive, but barely," Nancy said.

Ned knelt down beside her. "I bet whoever attacked her is going to be real disappointed to hear that."

83

"I don't know if Shannon was attacked," Nancy said. "But I *do* know that she's badly hurt. She might have decided to wait for Rafe on the pier, lost her footing in the darkness, and been knocked out when she fell onto the rocks."

Nancy moved her fingers gently to the back of Shannon's head and felt the stickiness of blood beneath her hair. "She's bleeding. She may have fractured her skull. She's probably also suffering from exposure after lying out here in the cold for so long," Nancy said. "We need to get her to a doctor right away. I saw lights on in the caretaker's cottage when we passed it on our way to the beach. We can phone for an ambulance from there. Do you think you can carry her that far?"

"No problem. She looks like a featherweight—probably why I thought it was Angie at first."

As Ned wrapped Shannon's heavy black coat more tightly around her, Nancy noticed something glinting in the dim light—tiny shards of glass from the shattered crystal of the watch the girl was wearing on her left wrist. Picking up Shannon's hand, Nancy saw that the watch had stopped at half-past twelve. The crystal must have broken on the rocks when Shannon fell, Nancy thought.

Ned scooped up Shannon's limp body and followed Nancy back the way they had come.

Light though Shannon was, his burden slowed him down. It seemed to take forever to reach the house where Soundview's caretaker lived. In response to Nancy's frantic knocking, a gray-haired man opened the door. He listened to her brief explanation of who she and Ned were and where they had found Shannon.

Peering at the white-faced girl in Ned's arms, he said, "She don't look too good. What happened to her, anyway?"

"We don't know, but she needs medical attention as soon as possible," Nancy said. "Can you please call an ambulance?"

"Better not," the man said. "No telling how long it'll take for one to get here. The nearest hospital's in Northville, and they're real understaffed. My station wagon's outside—I'll drive you there. I can't hang around, though. You'll have to get back on your own."

There were few cars on the road at that early hour on a Sunday morning. As they drove, Ned and Nancy spoke quietly.

"You don't really think this was an accident, do you?" Ned asked.

"I don't know," Nancy answered. "Like I said before, she might have decided to wait for Rafe on the pier, lost her footing in the dark, and been knocked out when she fell onto the rocks."

"That's a slim chance, Nan, if you ask me,"

Ned said, shaking his head. "This girl has too many enemies for accidents like this to just 'happen' to her."

"I agree," Nancy admitted. "But without evidence to the contrary, I'm not jumping to any conclusions."

There were no other patients in the emergency room when they arrived at the hospital twenty minutes later. Two orderlies removed Shannon from the car, and when they had wheeled her away on a gurney, the caretaker left.

After Nancy and Ned gave the woman at the admissions window what little information they had—Shannon's name and where they had found her—they went into the waiting room.

"We ought to try to contact Glenn MacInnes and tell him what's happened," Ned suggested. "Even though he and Shannon had that big fight last night, I bet he'd want to know."

"Why don't you call him? I noticed a pay phone next to the entrance when we came in."

Ned returned a few minutes later. "I got his number from directory assistance, but nobody picked up, so I left a message on his machine," he told Nancy. "Now I guess there's nothing else we can do except wait to hear what the doctor has to say."

They waited for what seemed like a very long

time. At last a tall, thin young man in surgical scrubs came over to them and introduced himself as Dr. Voorhees. He made it very clear that there was no question of Shannon's injury being accidental.

"Your friend is comatose due to a severe concussion caused by a blow to the back of the head with a heavy object of some kind," he said. "Whoever struck her meant business—it's a miracle she's still alive. Luckily, the X rays reveal no fracture of the skull. I've stitched the lacerations on her scalp, and I'll want to do a CAT scan to rule out the possibility of hemorrhage or blood clots on the brain. Naturally, we'll be keeping her under close observation in our neurological unit until she regains consciousness."

"Do you have any idea when that will be?" Nancy asked. "When she comes to, she might be able to identify the person who attacked her."

Dr. Voorhees shook his head. "Impossible to tell. In some cases, the patient recovers spontaneously with her mental faculties intact. In others, recovery is very slow and may be accompanied by amnesia. And in the worst-case scenario, the patient remains in a coma indefinitely," he said. "Because of the nature of the injury, I'll have to notify the authorities."

After the doctor returned to the treatment

room, Ned looked up the number of a local taxi service and ordered a car to pick them up.

As they waited for the taxi outside the hospital, Ned said, "This is really weird. All along, we've assumed that Angela's been in danger from Shannon, and now it's Shannon who turns out to be the victim."

"Which opens up a whole new can of worms," Nancy pointed out. "Shannon was the only person with a reason for wanting Angela out of the way, but there are *three* people with strong motives for getting rid of Shannon, and all of them knew exactly where to find her last night."

"Yeah. Maybe Glenn MacInnes didn't answer when I called because he's skipped town. He was definitely out of control last night— maybe furious enough to try to kill her," Ned said. "As for Rafe, we both heard him tell Angela that Shannon would never come between them again. By bumping Shannon off, he could make sure of that—*dead* sure."

"And then there's Angela herself," Nancy said.

Much as she hated to believe that their friend could be capable of harming anyone, even the girl she blamed for ruining her life, Angela was definitely a prime suspect. After the confrontation with Shannon at the country club, Angela had been close to the breaking point, and although Mr. Tremain had followed her when she left the estate, Angela had had a head start. She could easily have lost her stepfather on those narrow, winding roads if she was on her way to the Point with murder on her mind.

Ned's voice interrupted Nancy's thoughts. "So what do we tell the cops?"

"Nothing," she said. "At least, not until I have a chance to do some investigating on my own."

"You might not get that chance," Ned warned. "Now that Angela's called off the wedding, there's no reason for us to stay at Soundview any longer."

Nancy shook her head. "Wrong. Angela wanted us to come early because she was in trouble and needed our help. We can't abandon her now, when she's in even bigger trouble and needs us more than ever. You can go back to River Heights if you like, but I'm not leaving unless Angela asks me to."

"Okay, okay. I'm not going anywhere without you, Nan," Ned said quickly. "You know that." He hesitated, then added, "But there's something you ought to consider before you start trying to figure out who attacked Shannon. What if this investigation of yours backfires?"

"What do you mean?" Nancy asked.

"Well, you're assuming you'll be able to prove that Angela's innocent, and I sure hope you're right. But what if it doesn't work out that way? What if you discover evidence that proves the opposite?"

"I've thought about that," she said, "but no matter how bad things look right now, I can't bring myself to believe Angela would do something like this."

The taxi pulled up to the hospital entrance at that moment, and Nancy and Ned got inside. As they rode back to the estate, Nancy leaned her head tiredly against Ned's shoulder and said softly, "I sure hope Angela and her stepfather are at Soundview when we get there. As much as I believe Angela's innocent, she's still going to need an airtight alibi—and Mr. Tremain's the only one who can provide it."

When they arrived at Soundview, Parker let them in.

"Are Mr. Tremain and Angela back yet?" Nancy asked.

The butler seemed surprised. "I didn't know they'd gone out, Miss. I believe Mr. Tremain is in his study, but I haven't seen Miss Angela this morning."

At the sound of their voices, Mr. Tremain strode out into the hall, looking haggard and drawn. "Where have you two been?" he demanded. "Have you seen Angela?"

Nancy's heart sank. "No, Mr. Tremain, not

since last night. We thought she might be with you."

His broad shoulders sagged. "Please come into my study. We need to talk."

As soon as the study door closed behind them, Howard Tremain said, "I don't want to alarm anyone, but I gather you've discovered that Angela's missing. She left the grounds late last night, and she hasn't returned. I was terribly concerned about her, so I followed her."

"I know," Nancy said. "I saw both you and Angela leave."

"I followed her—and then I lost her." Mr. Tremain ran his hands through his silver hair in frustration. "One minute Angela's car was in plain sight, and the next it rounded a bend in the road and simply vanished. I drove all over the North Fork without finding a trace of her and only gave up about an hour ago. I was just about to call the police."

"Does Mrs. Tremain know that Angela's disappeared?" Ned asked.

"No!" Mr. Tremain exclaimed. "Felicia is still asleep, but when she wakes up, we must keep it from her at all costs. In her condition, I'm afraid she won't survive the shock." He drew a deep, shuddering breath. "If anything has happened to Angela, I'll never forgive myself."

Nancy had no words of comfort to offer. Her

THE NANCY DREW FILES

eyes met Ned's with an unspoken question. How could they tell Howard Tremain that they suspected that his stepdaughter, who was also their good friend, might have tried to murder Shannon Mulcahey?

The tense silence was shattered when the study door suddenly opened, and Angela burst into the room.

Chapter
Ten

AT THE SIGHT of her, Howard Tremain staggered backward and sank into the nearest chair. He seemed overcome with emotion. "Angela," he whispered. He was obviously even more relieved at Angela's return than Ned and she were; Nancy thought for a moment she feared he might actually pass out.

So did Angela. She had taken off her long black coat, and now she ran over to her stepfather and dropped to her knees in front of his chair.

"Howard, you look dreadful! Are you all right?" she cried anxiously.

When Mr. Tremain finally found his voice, it was a gravelly whisper that sounded nothing at all like his usual booming bass. "I'm fine, now that you're home," he rasped. "I've been driving all over the island looking for you. When you walked in that door just now, I was afraid I was hallucinating." Pulling himself together with great effort, he asked, "Where have you been all this time, Angela? I've been worried to death!"

"We all have," Nancy said.

Angela hung her head. "I'm so sorry," she murmured. "I didn't mean to upset you. I suppose I should have told somebody where I was going last night, but at the time I honestly didn't know. I guess it sounds weird, but I felt that if I drove far enough and fast enough, I could leave all my troubles behind. I was so miserable and confused about Rafe and Shannon that I wasn't thinking straight. But that's all over now. I've come to my senses."

She raised glowing eyes to her stepfather's. "I didn't believe you when you told me everything would work out for the best, but you were right. Rafe and I are going to be married after all. Isn't it wonderful?"

Nancy had thought she was prepared for whatever Angela might have to say, including a confession of murder, but this joyous announcement took her completely by surprise. She noticed that Mr. Tremain and Ned seemed equally stunned.

Angela looked from one astonished face to

another. "I—I thought you'd be happy for us," she faltered.

"Oh, we are," Ned said, recovering first. "That's great, but under the circumstances, you can't blame us for being kind of shocked."

"When did all this happen?" Nancy asked.

"Yes, Angela. You owe us an explanation. Tell us everything, from the time you drove away last night," Howard insisted.

Angela stood up. "Well, as I said before, I didn't have any idea where I was going at first, but the minute I got behind the wheel, I knew I had to find out if Rafe was going to meet Shannon at the Point, so that's where I went," she began. "I pulled my car off the road behind some trees, then sneaked down to a spot where I had a good view of the beach. It was very dark, but I could just make out Shannon standing on the pier. She was alone. I hid behind some big rocks and watched for a while, but no one else came.

"And then I suddenly realized how crazy I was acting, even crazier than Shannon, and how unfair I'd been to Rafe. I got back into the car and drove straight to his studio. I didn't know how he'd react to my turning up in the middle of the night like that after the way I'd treated him, but the minute we saw each other we knew everything would be all right. We've been talking all night." Angela's smile was radiant. "I love Rafe so much, and now I'm sure he loves me, too—surer than I've ever been about anything. This afternoon after we get some rest, we're going to see Shannon and make her face the truth. Maybe if she hears it from both of us, she'll finally leave us alone."

"I'm glad you and Rafe have made up," Nancy said quietly, "but I'm afraid you won't be able to speak to Shannon right now. She's in a coma. Someone attacked her last night."

Angela gasped, and Mr. Tremain leaned forward, gripping the arms of his chair so hard that his knuckles turned white. "What? How do you know this?" he demanded.

"Ned and I decided to walk down to the Point early this morning, and we found Shannon lying on the rocks by the pier," Nancy told him. "She was in pretty bad shape. Someone had struck her on the head, apparently with the intention of killing her."

"We brought her to your caretaker's cottage, and the caretaker drove us to Northville Hospital," Ned put in. "The doctor who treated Shannon in the emergency room said that it's too soon to tell when—or if—she'll regain consciousness."

Angela covered her face with her hands. "How horrible! Who could have done such a thing?"

"That's what I mean to find out," Nancy said. "This is really important, Angela. Do you know what time it was when you left the Point to go to Rafe's?"

"Quarter after twelve," Angela said promptly.

"Are you absolutely sure of that?"

"Yes, because I checked my watch just before I headed back to my car. I arrived at Rafe's studio about ten minutes later." She frowned. "I don't get it, Nancy. Why is the time so important?"

"Shannon was wearing a watch, too," Nancy said. "The crystal was broken, and the watch had stopped at twelve-thirty. It must have happened when she fell onto the rocks from the pier."

"But what does that have to do with Rafe and me?" Angela asked.

"Everything," Nancy said. "Don't you see? If you were with Rafe at his place then, you're both in the clear."

Angela stared at her in dismay. "Of course we are! You didn't actually suspect either of us of attacking Shannon, did you, Nancy?"

"I'd certainly hoped you both had nothing to do with it. But passions have been flying pretty high around here lately. And passion has been known to make even the nicest people do the most unlikely things.

"But," Nancy continued, thinking aloud, "now that I can eliminate you and Rafe as possible suspects, Glenn is the only person who had both motive and opportunity for attacking Shannon Mulcahey."

"Then I suggest you go to the police immediately and tell them about his violent behavior at the country club," Mr. Tremain said. "The sooner he's locked up, the better for all concerned!"

There was obviously very little crime in Port Wellington, Nancy thought, since the police department didn't even have its own building. It occupied one wing of the firehouse on Maple Street.

As Nancy and Ned entered the station, Nancy looked around. The only officer on duty was a middle-aged man sitting behind the front desk. He was reading a newspaper and drinking coffee from a foam cup. The name plate on the desk identified him as Sergeant Pulaski.

The officer looked up without much interest as Nancy approached the counter. "What's up?" he asked wearily. "Lost pet? Stolen bicycle? Fender-bender?" He took a piece of paper from a pile on his desk and shoved it across the counter. "Fill out the form. Whatever it is, we'll look into it."

"I'm afraid it's more serious than that, officer," Ned said.

"We're here because we have some important information about the girl who was attacked last night at Rocky Point," Nancy told him. "I believe Dr. Voorhees of Northville Hospital filed a report a few hours ago."

That got the sergeant's attention. He quickly put down his newspaper and sat up in his chair. "You mean Shannon Mulcahey. That's a bad business, all right. My son used to date her back in high school. Beautiful girl, but wild, really wild." He shook his head. "Seems like that girl was always asking for trouble."

Sergeant Pulaski took their names, then asked, "What do you know about the incident?"

"We're staying at Soundview, the Chamberlain estate," Ned explained. "While we were taking a walk down the beach to the Point earlier this morning, we found Shannon on the rocks by the pier. She was unconscious, so I carried her to the caretaker's cottage. He drove us to the hospital, where Dr. Voorhees treated her."

"We've got a pretty good idea of who did it, and when," Nancy added. She began by telling the officer about the altercation at the Port Wellington Country Club the previous night and Glenn's part in it, but when she went on to describe how she had established the time of the attack by Shannon's broken watch, Sergeant Pulaski cut her off.

"Forget it, miss. If you're right and Shannon was hit at twelve-thirty, there's no way MacInnes could have done it."

Ned frowned. "How come?"

"Because the guy wrapped his truck around a tree on Country Club Road at"—the sergeant punched some keys on his computer and peered at the monitor—"ten forty-six. That's when we found him and got him to Northville Hospital."

"That doesn't necessarily mean Glenn's out of the picture," Nancy argued. "If he was treated and released, there still would have been time for him to drive to the Point shortly after midnight."

"Yes, there would, *if* that was what happened, but it's not," Sergeant Pulaski said. "In the first place, his truck was totaled. And in the second place, according to the EMS report, he has a fractured clavicle and possible internal injuries. He was kept in the hospital for observation."

The sergeant looked at Nancy over his glasses. "Let me ask you this. Was there anyone else involved in that nasty business at the country club last night, anyone who might have known Shannon would be at the Point later that night?"

Nancy shook her head. "No, no one else."

He turned off his computer and leaned back in his chair. "Well, thanks for stopping by. I appreciate the information, but I'm afraid it doesn't do us any good. If you think of anything else that might be important, let me know. Sooner or later we'll find out who attacked Shannon Mulcahey."

Her case had just taken a decidedly odd turn, Nancy thought as she and Ned left the police station. She was completely baffled, and it was a feeling she definitely didn't like.

Chapter
Eleven

NANCY, IT LOOKS like you're fresh out of suspects," Ned said as he got behind the wheel of the Corvette, and Nancy climbed into the passenger side.

"It's driving me nuts!" Nancy pounded her fist on the dashboard in frustration. "If Glenn didn't attack Shannon, then who did?"

"Nan, did you ever stop to think her attack might have been a random act of violence? Unfortunately, it happens all the time, no matter how exclusive the area is. Obviously, Soundview is no exception."

Nancy shook her head. "Normally I'd agree with you, but there are too many elements of this case that I don't believe are random or coincidental. I plan on finding out who attacked Shannon if it's the last thing I do."

"Why?" Ned put his arm around her shoulders. "Take it easy, Nan. This really isn't your problem, you know. You're not the detective on this case. It was one thing when we thought Angela or Rafe might have been involved, but now we know they're not. Shannon may have been a threat to Angela before, but she isn't anymore, and the wedding's back on. How about concentrating on being a bridesmaid from now on and letting the cops take it from here?"

"I guess my ego's a little bruised," Nancy confessed. "I just can't believe I can't unravel this one. But you're right—it's up to the cops to discover who tried to murder Shannon Mulcahey." She sighed. "I can't help feeling sorry for Shannon, but I certainly am thankful that it wasn't Angela we found."

"When I first saw the body, I was sure it was Angie," Ned said. "They were both wearing black coats last night, and they're about the same height and build. I bet if you saw them together from the back, it would be hard to tell one from the other. I guess Rafe really goes for small, dark-haired girls." He pulled Nancy closer and murmured in her ear, "Personally, I prefer tall, beautiful blonds."

Nancy stiffened. "What did you just say?"

"Fishing for compliments, huh?" Ned teased. "I said I prefer—"

"Not that. What was it you said about Angela and Shannon?"

"You mean that from the back it would be hard to tell one from the other?"

"That's it," Nancy whispered. "And on a dark, moonless night it would be almost impossible. Oh, Ned, what if that's what happened? What if whoever attacked her made a mistake, and it was *Angela,* not Shannon, who was supposed to be the victim?"

"I hate to say this, Nan, but I think you might be overthinking this," Ned said. "Angela's only enemy was Shannon. She was the one who sent her all that junk—the china, the clipping, and the letter—and messed up the straps of her saddle girth."

"We can't be sure about the girth," Nancy objected. "When Angela accused her last night, Shannon said she didn't know anything about it, remember? Why would she have denied that when she actually boasted about being responsible for the other incidents?"

"Well, maybe because fiddling with someone's saddle with the intent to hurt them crosses the line into criminal behavior. But, frankly, right now, I'm too tired to care."

Ned removed his arm from around her and started the car. As he pulled away from the curb and drove down the street, he said, "We're both pretty strung out. It's been a rough night, and neither of us has had a whole lot of sleep in the past forty-eight hours. I don't know about you, but my brain's not firing on all cylinders right now. Let's just get something to eat and catch some zees, okay?"

Nancy was exhausted and hungry, too, but on the way back to Soundview her brain, unlike Ned's, was working overtime. If the target of Shannon's would-be murderer had indeed been Angela, he must have discovered his mistake by now. With no evidence to connect him to the crime, Nancy figured he wouldn't hesitate to strike again, and that meant that Angela was still in grave danger. She was more determined than ever to discover that person's identity, with Ned's help or without it.

When they arrived at the house, Nancy saw an unfamiliar car was parked on the circular drive. "Oh, no!" Nancy exclaimed as she noted the license plate. "That's a doctor's license plate" she said to Ned. "Something terrible must have happened."

Parker let them in. In response to her anxious question, he replied, "I'm sorry to tell you that Mrs. Tremain collapsed shortly after breakfast, Miss Drew. Miss Angela called Dr. Harvey, and the doctor is with Mrs. Tremain now."

"But last night at the dance, she seemed so much better," Nancy said.

Parker nodded sadly. "I'm sure you and Mr.

Nickerson remember as well as we do what she was like before she became ill—so active, so full of energy, and now . . ." For an instant the butler's composure faltered, but he quickly recovered. After taking their coats, he said, "Mr. Tremain and Miss Angela have already eaten, but Mr. Tremain instructed me to tell the cook when you returned. I will do so at once. If you will proceed to the breakfast room, brunch will be ready momentarily."

Nancy and Ned were soon served eggs Benedict, freshly squeezed orange juice, fruit compote, and steaming hot coffee. Although the meal was delicious and they were both starving, they were both too worried about Felicia to appreciate it.

Nancy was also concerned about Angela. She was convinced that their friend's life was in danger, but the pieces of the puzzle she'd assembled so far didn't form a picture that made any sense.

Who aside from Shannon stood to benefit from Angela's death? There had to be someone else, someone whose motives Nancy knew nothing about. . . .

Alice, one of the maids, came into the room, interrupting her thoughts. "Miss Drew, your father is on the line." She held out a cordless phone.

Nancy had forgotten that when she had spoken to her father before she left for New York, he'd said he would call her on Sunday. Maybe he could shed some light on the situation.

"Thank you, Alice." She took the phone. "Hi, Dad. How are things in Seattle?"

"Wet," her father grumbled. "It's been raining ever since I got here. I think I'm developing a case of terminal mildew. The trial is proceeding fairly rapidly, however. With any luck, I should be able to make Angela's wedding. What about you, Nancy? Are you and Ned having fun?"

Nancy grimaced. *"Fun* isn't exactly the word for it, Dad. Things have been pretty hairy since we got here."

When she had finished giving him a brief rundown of the events of the past few days, Mr. Drew said, "I see what you mean. Since the Mulcahey girl can't be considered a suspect any longer, what other leads are you pursuing?"

"I've been trying to figure out who else might have a reason for wanting Angela out of the way, and as you know, greed is one of the strongest motives of all," Nancy replied. "Angela comes into her inheritance from her father next month when she turns twenty-one. I know you and Gordon Chamberlain were close friends. Did he ever happen to mention who would benefit if Angela died *before* her twenty-first birthday?"

"As a matter of fact, he did, but I'm afraid it won't be of any use to you," her father said. "In that case, Angela's inheritance passes to her mother."

Nancy sighed. "You're right. That doesn't get me anywhere."

They talked for a few more minutes. Then Mr. Drew rang off, and Nancy set the cordless phone down on the table.

"What did your dad say?" Ned asked.

"Well, he didn't have any helpful information about Mr. Chamberlain's will. He said in the event of Angela's death, the inheritance would go to Angela's mother. But even if Mrs. Tremain wasn't so ill, she'd be above suspicion, don't you think?"

"Absolutely," Ned agreed.

Nancy rubbed her forehead. Her head was throbbing as though it were about to split in two. In spite of the coffee she had drunk, a wave of exhaustion passed over her, and she slumped in a chair.

Ned got up and pulled her to her feet. "Come on, Nan. Time to catch those zees. If we don't get some sleep, we're both going to be basket cases—and no use to Angela or anyone else."

Nancy was too tired to argue. Her sleepless nights and frantic days had finally caught up with her, and the thought of falling into bed, if only for a little while, was irresistible. After a brief doze, she would focus all her energies on tracking down Angela's unknown enemy, even though, with Shannon out of the picture, it meant starting over from scratch.

As Nancy and Ned left the breakfast room, they ran into Mr. Tremain, who had just seen Dr. Harvey to the door. He told them that according to the doctor, there was no cause for alarm. Felicia had simply overtaxed her strength by attending the dinner dance. She was resting comfortably now, and Angela, relieved that her mother was feeling better, had gone to bed also. He asked about what had happened at the police station.

"Nothing," Ned replied. "Nothing that did any good, anyway."

"An officer took our statement, but it turns out that Glenn MacInnes totaled his truck right after he drove away from the club last night," Nancy added. "He was taken straight to the hospital, so he couldn't have been responsible for the attack on Shannon."

"So you're saying that whoever attacked her is still at large?" Mr. Tremain asked. "That *is* distressing. Let's hope the police find the attacker before someone else is hurt. Well, Nancy, at least you and Ned have the satisfaction of knowing you've done everything you could to discover his identity."

Nancy shook her aching head. "Not yet, but I

will. You see, Mr. Tremain, I've come to the conclusion that we've been barking up the wrong tree. I believe it was Angela who was supposed to be the victim, and I intend to prove it by shifting the focus of my investigation to any enemies Angela might have."

"Angela has no enemies!" Mr. Tremain said sharply. "That's nonsense!" Then his tone softened. "Forgive me, Nancy. I didn't mean to snap at you, but it seems a bit far-fetched that Shannon was attacked by somebody who thought she was Angela."

"I'm inclined to agree with you, sir," Ned admitted with an apologetic glance at Nancy.

"In my opinion, Shannon Mulcahey was probably a victim of the ugly random violence that is all too common these days," Mr. Tremain went on. "Even in an exclusive area like this, no one is completely safe. I understand that some very undesirable characters—drifters, homeless people—have been spotted around the village recently. Unfortunately, even if the girl eventually comes to, she probably won't be able to identify her assailant since she was struck from behind. I'm sure our local police will do everything they can, but it's possible that the culprit will never be found."

Nancy listened to Mr. Tremain through a fog of weariness. Although she remained unconvinced, she was too tired to argue with her host or with Ned. She just murmured something noncommittal and plodded up the stairs to her room.

Without even bothering to take off her clothes, Nancy flopped down on the bed. But exhausted though she was, she couldn't fall asleep immediately. Something was bothering her, something she had seen or heard that didn't ring true, but she was much too groggy to figure out what it was.

Chapter
Twelve

NANCY WOKE UP two hours later, feeling refreshed after a deep, dreamless sleep. Looking out one of her bedroom windows, she saw that heavy clouds had gathered overhead, promising more snow. It would be a white Christmas for sure, but not a merry one if what she suspected was true and Angela's life was still in danger.

As she splashed cold water on her face and combed her tangled hair, Nancy's thoughts kept returning to Angela's fall in the riding ring and the mystery of the saddle girth. There was no doubt in her mind that the girth had been tampered with, but Nancy still believed that Shannon had been telling the truth when she'd said she knew nothing about it. Was there someone else who might have had access to the stable's tack room? The first phase of Nancy's investigation would be to question Norris. When she had packed her suitcase for the trip to Soundview, she'd tucked her miniature tape recorder inside, and she decided she would take it with her to record what Norris had to say.

The second phase would be to return to the scene of the crime.

When Nancy and Ned had found Shannon in the early hours of that morning, Nancy's chief concern had been to get her to a doctor as soon as possible. There hadn't been time to scour the area around the pier for clues to the identify of Shannon's assailant. As for the Port Wellington police, Sergeant Pulaski had said nothing about their checking out the Point at all. Even if they had, Nancy knew from past experience that they might have overlooked some vital piece of evidence. If so, she was determined to find it.

Nancy stepped out of her room into the corridor. Angela's door was closed, and so was Ned's. Apparently they were still asleep, but to make sure that Angela hadn't pulled another disappearing act, Nancy very quietly turned the knob of her door, opening it just far enough to allow her to see that her friend was indeed sleeping peacefully in her canopied bed.

The huge house was eerily silent as Nancy tiptoed down the broad staircase to the first floor. There was no sign of Mr. Tremain or the servants. She took her jacket from the closet where Parker had hung it earlier, dropped the recorder into a pocket, and slipped out the front door.

Once outside, Nancy broke into a brisk jog and reached the stable a few minutes later. A beat-up beige sedan that Nancy had not seen before was parked next to the stable yard. Hoping that the car belonged to Norris, she entered the stable, but the red-haired young man coming out of the feed room definitely wasn't Norris. Maybe he was Shannon's cousin.

"Hi. Are you Jeremy?" Nancy asked.

"No, I'm Sean. Jeremy doesn't work here anymore." Sean glowered at her suspiciously. "Who're you?"

"Nancy Drew, a guest of Angela Chamberlain. My friend Ned and I came to Soundview for her wedding," Nancy replied. She walked over to Ranger's stall and stroked the chestnut gelding's nose. "Ranger and I are old pals."

Sean's hostility vanished. "That's okay then. I didn't mean to be rude, but Mr. Tremain doesn't like strangers hanging around the stable. Do you want to ride? I can saddle Ranger for you."

"Not today, thanks." Turning on the tape recorder concealed in her pocket, Nancy asked, "When did Jeremy quit?"

"He didn't quit. The boss fired him a couple of months ago," Sean told her. "Jeremy was really mad at Mr. Tremain and Angela, too, because he blamed her for blowing the whistle on him. But if you ask me, he deserved it. Jeremy Dowd had a bad attitude, always walking around with a chip on his shoulder. He was also lazy and rough with the horses."

"Funny," Nancy said. "Angela never mentioned anything about him."

Sean shrugged. "She probably didn't even know his name. Jeremy was only here for a short while, and part-time at that. Did you want to speak to him?"

"No. Just curious, that's all. Actually, I was looking for Norris."

"Afraid you're out of luck," Sean said. "Sunday is Norris's day off. I come in a couple of times to check on the horses and give them their feed. Then I lock up and go home."

"Is the stable always locked when nobody's here?" Nancy asked.

"Yeah, at least ever since some animal-rights nuts went around 'liberating' the horses on the North Fork about a year ago and a lot of valuable animals were lost or injured. That's when the boss beefed up security measures. He even had an alarm system installed."

"Sounds like a good idea."

Nancy went from Ranger's stall to Starlight's. "I know how upset Angela would be if anything happened to her mare. By the way, Sean, were you around on Friday when Angela was thrown?"

He shook his head. "I was off that day, but I heard about it. Boy, was she ever lucky! She could've been paralyzed, or even killed. Norris was all shook up about it, especially when the boss acted like it was his fault. But it wasn't. That girth wasn't worn, like Mr. Tremain said. Norris takes real good care of all the tack."

"What happened to the girth? Is it still around?" Nancy asked casually.

"No. The boss took it with him after he yelled at Norris—said he wanted to make sure it was never used again. I guess he probably threw it out."

"I see. Well, nice talking with you, Sean." Nancy gave Starlight a final pat, then headed for the door.

"If you still want to see Norris, he'll be back at work tomorrow," Sean called after her.

"Thanks. Maybe I'll stop by," Nancy said.

As she started back to the house, she thought about what Sean had said. Considering the security measures he had described, it would be just about impossible for any unauthorized person to enter the stable without being detected.

But someone who had previously worked there—Jeremy Dowd, for instance—could have retained a set of keys and might also know how to override the alarm. Had he been angry enough at Angela to try to harm her? It was a long shot, but Nancy decided that she would try to find out more about him from Norris on Monday. Right now, however, she wanted to check out the Point while there were still several hours of daylight left.

A few flakes of snow had begun to fall as Nancy walked up the path from the stable to the house. She planned on taking the Corvette, which was still parked on the drive where Ned had left it, but when she reached into her jeans pocket for the car keys, they weren't there. It was only then that she remembered she'd given them to Ned that morning so he could drive to the police station.

For a moment Nancy thought about waking him to get the keys back, but then changed her mind. He was exhausted, and she didn't want to disturb him. She decided she'd walk instead.

Nancy was retracing her steps around the driveway when she heard a deep voice calling, "Nancy? Is that you?"

When she stopped and turned around, she saw Angela's stepfather coming out the front door.

"Yes, it's me, Mr. Tremain."

Mr. Tremain strode over to her. "I'm surprised that you're up and about so soon. After all you've been through, I thought you'd be enjoying a well-earned rest. Where are you off to?"

Nancy hesitated. Like Ned, Mr. Tremain had made it clear that he thought her renewed fears for Angela were totally off the wall. If she told him what she had in mind, he would probably try to talk her out of it.

Well, no matter how hard he tries, he won't succeed, Nancy thought. Mr. Tremain may not approve, but he can't very well forbid me to leave the estate.

Aloud she said, "I'm going to take a walk to Rocky Point. I want to see if I can turn up any clues to the identity of the person who attacked Shannon last night."

"I gather you still think the person who attacked Shannon mistook her for Angela." Mr. Tremain smiled. "You don't give up easily, do you, Nancy?"

"No, I don't," Nancy agreed.

"Good for you! Perseverance is a fine quality, but unless it's combined with a certain amount of caution, it can sometimes lead to disaster."

"I'm not sure I know what you mean, Mr. Tremain," Nancy said.

"Simply that going off by yourself on a sleuthing expedition could be dangerous, particularly in a situation like this," Mr. Tremain replied. "After what happened to the Mulcahey girl, I don't think it's safe for a young woman to wander around an isolated area like the Point alone."

"I appreciate your concern, Mr. Tremain, but honestly, I'm pretty good at taking care of myself," Nancy replied. "I have to be in my line of work."

"No doubt you are, but as your host, your safety is my responsibility. As I mentioned earlier, some very unsavory characters have been seen recently in the vicinity of Port Wellington. One of them might have assaulted Shannon and could attack you as well. I can't prevent you from going to the Point, Nancy, but if you're determined to do this thing, I insist on driving you there."

Although the last thing Nancy wanted or needed was a baby-sitter, she couldn't think of a polite way to refuse Mr. Tremain's offer. Besides, the snow was coming down harder now. If she walked to the Point as she had originally intended, by the time she got there, it would be much more difficult to discover the evidence she sought.

Nancy smiled. "Thanks. I appreciate it." She followed Mr. Tremain around the side of the house to where his Mercedes was parked, then got in and buckled herself into the passenger seat. As Mr. Tremain drove through Soundview's grounds, she was deep in thought. If only she could make sense of the shifting puzzle this case had become! Although Nancy intended to follow up on the lead Sean had supplied when he told her about Jeremy, she doubted it would come to much. Meanwhile, she racked her brain, trying to think of what it was that had been nagging at her just before she fell asleep.

And all of a sudden it came to her.

That morning when Howard Tremain had referred to the attack on Shannon, he'd said that he doubted she would be able to identify her assailant because he had struck her from behind. But neither Nancy nor Ned had told him that. They had only remarked that Shannon had been hit on the head.

How could Mr. Tremain have known—unless he'd been there?

Chapter

Thirteen

IT WAS SUCH an astonishing thought that Nancy was stunned. She felt as though the breath had been knocked out of her body, and her heart was pounding so wildly that she imagined Mr. Tremain must be able to hear it.

Get a grip! Nancy commanded herself. It's just not possible!

If Howard Tremain was at the Point the night before and had witnessed the attack on Shannon, he would certainly have said so. The alternative—that he himself had tried to murder her, thinking she was Angela—was too utterly fantastic to be considered, even for a moment.

There had to be some mistake! Maybe Nancy was confused about what she had heard. During her brief conversation with Mr. Tremain in the hall at Soundview that morning before she and Ned had gone to their rooms, she had been so tired that she was on the verge of collapse. In her exhaustion she might very well have misunderstood what Angela's stepfather said.

Closing her eyes tightly, Nancy forced herself to concentrate and call up the scene. In her mind's eye Nancy pictured herself, Ned, and Angela's stepfather as clearly as though they were on a video screen, and she heard every word Howard Tremain had spoken in his deep, resonant voice: "Unfortunately, even if the girl eventually comes to, she probably won't be able to identify her assailant, since she was struck from behind."

She shuddered. If there had been a mistake, it was Mr. Tremain's, not hers!

Angela's stepfather turned his attention from the road to glance at her. "Nancy, are you all right? You're shivering, and you don't look well. Perhaps we'd better turn back. You can pursue your investigation tomorrow when you're more rested."

Nancy opened her eyes. "I'm fine," she said, hoping she sounded normal.

But she wasn't fine at all. As she sat rigid in her seat and stared out the windshield, other vivid images flooded her mind. Nancy remembered Mr. Tremain's original dismissal of her theory about Angela's riding "accident," although later he seemed convinced that she was right. Had he been a little too eager to place the blame for the weakened saddle girth first on Norris and then on Shannon? Also, just a short while ago in the stable, Sean told Nancy that Mr. Tremain had taken the girth away. Why had he done that? Was it because he didn't want anyone to discover that the straps *had* been cut?

And then there was his extreme reaction earlier that morning when Angela had come into the study. At the time Nancy saw no reason to doubt his word when he'd said that after spending hours searching for Angela, he was overcome with relief at her safe return. But now . . .

While Nancy still believed that an enemy of Angela had attacked her, she had never for a moment suspected Angela's stepfather. But things had changed. Howard Tremain claimed he'd driven around looking for Angela. What if, instead of losing sight of Angela when he had driven after her as he said, Mr. Tremain had followed her to Rocky Point? If he was under the impression that it was Angela he had left for dead on the rocks below the pier, no wonder he'd been in a state of shock when she turned up alive and unharmed.

Nancy pressed both hands to her throbbing temples. Mr. Tremain loved Angela. Why would he wish her—or Shannon or anyone else—any harm?

And yet the fact remained that he knew how Shannon had been injured, which placed him at the scene of the crime, and he had said nothing about it. There simply had to be a reasonable explanation for his silence, Nancy thought, one that would set her mind at rest once and for all.

She decided there was no point in beating around the bush. Turning to Angela's stepfather, she said, "Mr. Tremain, there's something I need to ask you."

He smiled. "Please do."

Okay here goes, Nancy thought. "Why didn't you tell anyone that you were at Rocky Point last night?"

Mr. Tremain's eyebrows shot up. "Whatever gave you the idea that I was at the Point?"

"When we were talking about Shannon Mulcahey this morning, you mentioned that someone had struck her from behind," Nancy said. "Unless you were there, you couldn't have known that."

They had left the estate by now, and as they drove along a narrow, winding road that paralleled the coastline, Nancy held her breath, waiting for Howard Tremain's reply. It was a long time in coming, and when he finally spoke, his words chilled her to the bone.

"You're right, of course," he said calmly. "I realized my error immediately, but I managed to convince myself that you were much too tired to pick up on it. That was very foolish of me. In spite of all Angela and her mother have told me about your sleuthing skills, it's obvious that I underestimated your talents. You were right about Starlight's saddle girth, too. Angela seems to lead a charming life. When I came home on Friday evening, I fully expected to discover that she'd had a fatal fall."

Mr. Tremain shook his head ruefully. "You're a very clever girl, Nancy, perhaps too clever for your own good. And I thought I had covered my tracks so well! I was so sure that no one, not even the famous detective Nancy Drew, would ever figure out that it was Angela, not Shannon, who was supposed to die last night."

Nancy stared at him in horror. She couldn't have been more appalled if Dr. Jekyll had turned into Mr. Hyde right before her eyes.

"Then it *was* you," she whispered. "It was you all along! But *why*, Mr. Tremain? Why did you try to kill Angela?"

To her astonishment, the man actually smiled. It was the same warm, gentle smile that had charmed Nancy ever since they first met.

Now, however, there was a sinister edge to that smile that made her blood run cold.

"So many questions!" he said with an exaggerated sigh. "Well, I'll try to keep it brief." Still smiling, he leaned back in the driver's seat and focused on the road ahead.

"It's basically a matter of economics," he began. "Galaxy Computers, which as you know, my late partner Gordon Chamberlain founded many years ago, has not been as successful since I took over as it was when Gordon was at the helm. In fact, the company is on the verge of bankruptcy. This regrettable state of affairs, you understand," he added quickly, "is a result of the current unfavorable business climate, *not* from any fault of my own. If Galaxy goes under, however, my reputation in the business community will be utterly destroyed. I will be powerless, a failure. Naturally, I can't allow such a thing to happen."

Nancy had listened in growing confusion. "What does all this have to do with Angela?" she asked.

"I'm coming to that," he replied. "A large—a *very* large—infusion of cash will be needed within the next few months to keep Galaxy afloat, and Angela is a very rich young woman who will become even wealthier when she comes into her inheritance."

"You mean you'd actually *murder* your step-daughter for money?" Nancy gasped. "You'd never get your hands on it, not in a million years! When I spoke to my father on the phone today, he told me that according to the terms of Mr. Chamberlain's will, if Angela dies before she turns twenty-one, her fortune goes to her mother."

Mr. Tremain nodded. "You're right. But you know, Felicia is so very ill, and her decline seems more rapid every day. . . ." He looked at Nancy gravely, raised an eyebrow, and then smiled.

The last piece of the puzzle had fallen into place, forming a picture that was far uglier than Nancy could ever have imagined. Howard Tremain was responsible for his own wife's illness—he must be poisoning her! She felt sick with revulsion. This was a nightmare—worse than a nightmare because it was real!

Desperate to grasp at any straw that might save her friend's life, as well as her mother's, Nancy said, "But if both Angela and her mother die under mysterious circumstances and you're the only person who benefits, suspicion is bound to fall on you, Mr. Tremain. What will happen to your precious reputation when you're indicted on a double murder charge?"

"Come now, Nancy. You of all people must

know that an indictment doesn't always result in a conviction, especially when the defendant can afford the finest lawyers in the country." Mr. Tremain glanced at her and grinned. "Who knows? Carson Drew might even be willing to take my case—*after* he recovers from the unfortunate death of his brilliant daughter!"

Chapter

Fourteen

ALTHOUGH NANCY WAS trembling inside, she refused to give Howard Tremain the satisfaction of seeing her flinch. Three lives were at stake—Angela's, Felicia Tremain's, and her own. She mustn't lose her cool.

How could she have been so wrong about Howard Tremain? Nancy wondered. It wasn't surprising that Angela and her mother had been taken in by his pose of loving stepfather and husband. After all, he had been Gordon Chamberlain's partner and a friend of the family for years. But Nancy's experience in dealing with criminals, thieves, and liars should have made her more wary. If only she'd seen what a monster was hiding behind that kindly mask!

Well, he's ripped off the mask now, she thought, and if I don't play my cards right, that handsome, evil face may be the last thing I'll ever see!

Nancy was furious at herself for being so gullible, and her anger sharpened her wits. She had learned that all egomaniacs loved to talk about themselves, and Howard Tremain was no exception. If she could just keep him talking long enough, she might be able to figure out how to get away.

Matching his casual tone, Nancy said, "Exactly how do you intend to get rid of me, Mr. Tremain? No matter what method you choose, you'll never get away with it, you know."

"Oh, I wouldn't be so sure about that," he said. "Felicia, Angela, and your friend Ned are all still asleep. As for Parker and the other servants, I gave them the afternoon off to go Christmas shopping in the village. Nobody could have seen us leave the house together. The first part of the statement I'll make to the police after I 'discover' your body is absolutely true. I'll inform them that when I looked into your room and found it empty, I became concerned. You left the door open, by the way," he added. "I hope you realize that I would never intrude on the privacy of my guests."

"How considerate!" Nancy muttered.

Howard Tremain continued, ignoring Nancy's sarcasm. "Then I'll say that I remembered hearing you mention that you intended to pursue your investigation of the attack on Shannon Mulcahey, and I guessed that you had returned to Rocky Point to search for clues. Convinced that the unfortunate Mulcahey girl had been attacked by some deranged drifter who might still be lurking somewhere near the scene, I feared for your safety and drove there myself. To my great distress, I arrived too late to save your life."

"Then you're planning a repeat performance of last night?"

"Not quite. Practice makes perfect, or so I've heard. I've learned from my previous mistakes. You'll be unconscious when you fall from the end of the pier where the water is deep, and then you'll drown."

While Howard Tremain was speaking, Nancy had been frantically scanning the road ahead for another vehicle. If she saw one, her plan was to get the driver's attention by seizing the wheel and forcing the Mercedes to swerve into the stone wall that ran along the roadside. Nancy was sure no motorist would be able to ignore an accident that took place right in front of him, and once they were no longer alone, Angela's stepfather would be unable to carry out his murderous scheme. The risk of injury in a crash was minor compared to what he had in mind for her.

But no car came. The road was deserted, and

the last house Nancy had seen was the cottage of Soundview's caretaker more than a mile back. She was completely on her own, trapped with the man who wanted her dead.

They were now approaching the turnoff to Rocky Point. As Howard slowed down to make the turn, Nancy took a desperate chance. She reached for the door handle, intending to make a run for it, but although she struggled with all her might, the door refused to open.

"Oh, Nancy," Mr. Tremain said. "I once underestimated you, and now it seems you've underestimated me. The locks on these doors can be controlled by the driver, a safety feature that I never had occasion to use until now."

He pulled off the unpaved lane and stopped the Mercedes in a grove of bare, twisted trees on the edge of the bluff overlooking the sound. As he got out and came around to the passenger side, Nancy tensed every muscle, ready to spring at him the instant he unlocked her door. Howard Tremain was strong and physically fit, but so was Nancy, and she was also less than half his age. Although she had no weapon, Nancy was an expert in self-defense. If she could catch Tremain off guard this time, she was sure she could immobilize him with a swift blow.

When his key turned in the lock, Nancy flung

open the door and leaped out, primed for the attack, but Tremain was too quick for her. He grabbed her upraised arm, wrenching it behind her back so viciously that Nancy couldn't suppress a sharp cry of pain.

"I'm disappointed in you, Nancy. That was very foolish," he growled. "For your own sake, I strongly advise you not to attempt anything like it again, or your death will be a much more lingering and agonizing one than I had originally intended."

There was no longer any trace of courtliness or humor in his manner, and as Nancy gazed into Howard Tremain's glittering eyes, she fought off a surge of pure panic. The man wasn't merely ruthless; he was totally insane.

Still holding on to her arm, Tremain shoved Nancy roughly ahead of him down the path that sloped from the top of the bluff to the beach. She slipped and slithered on the frozen ground, almost blinded by snow blown by an icy wind that had suddenly sprung up. It whipped across the sound, churning its waters into huge, ocean-size waves that broke on the rocky shore and battered the decrepit pier with a sound like thunder.

Once they were on the beach, Tremain forced Nancy in the direction of the pier. She knew it would be useless to struggle—Angela's stepfather was a lot stronger than she'd thought. Although she'd failed so far, Nancy's only hope of survival lay in outsmarting him.

Nancy and Howard Tremain stepped onto the pier. The crashing waves drenched them both with spray. It made the rotting boards and crumbling masonry underfoot so treacherous that Nancy stumbled several times.

And suddenly she had an idea.

It's now or never, she thought grimly.

She stumbled again, deliberately this time, and fell to her knees, pulling Tremain down with her. Taken completely by surprise, he released his grasp on her arm. Nancy scrambled to her feet only seconds before he did, but those seconds were all she needed to give her the advantage. When Tremain lunged at her, his face contorted with rage and his powerful hands reaching for her throat, she was ready for him.

With a quick shift of her weight, Nancy deftly threw him off balance. She then turned to face him squarely, and with a special twist of the waist and arms that she'd learned from her Japanese instructor in martial arts, she turned him over her shoulder and flung him to the ground.

Tremain lay very still. Nancy knelt down beside him, and when she checked his vital signs, she found that he was merely unconscious. Next, she searched the pockets of his heavy sheepskin coat and found his car keys. She would have to drive the Mercedes back to Soundview to call the police—there was no phone in Howard's car.

While Nancy was fighting for her life, she had been unaware of anything except the man who menaced her. Now that the nightmare was over and she was safe at last, she noticed that the snow had almost stopped, but the wind was still blowing. Nancy shivered violently. Although her jacket had somewhat protected her, her jeans were soaked from the crashing waves, and her hair was dripping. She was freezing cold. The arm Howard Tremain had twisted throbbed as she stood up and started walking back across the snowy beach.

Nancy was on her way up the path when she thought she heard someone calling her name— or was it just the howling of the wind?

"Nancy! Are you all right?"

It was Ned's voice! When she reached the top of the bluff, he ran to meet her. He hugged her close, almost squeezing the breath out of her. It hurt her injured arm, but Nancy was so glad to see him that she didn't care.

"How did you know where to find me?" she exclaimed.

"I didn't. It was just a lucky guess," Ned said. "When I looked out my bedroom window and saw you drive off with Mr. Tremain, I figured he'd be taking you here to scout around for clues. I was kind of surprised, though, since he thought your mistaken-identity theory was all wet—" He broke off. "Hey, *you're* all wet! What happened?"

Looking over his shoulder, Nancy saw the red Corvette parked next to Howard's Mercedes. The Corvette had a phone!

"I'll explain everything later," she promised, "but right now, I have to call the Port Wellington police."

"The police?" Ned echoed. "How come? What's going on?"

He followed Nancy to the car. She grabbed the phone and dialed 911, and when Ned heard what she told the officer who answered, his eyes widened in amazement.

"The cops are on their way," she said as she rang off.

"You're something else, Nancy," Ned said. "I can't believe you actually found the guy who attacked Shannon Mulcahey and knocked him out!"

"You're *really* not going to believe it when I tell you who the guy is," she said.

"You mean it's someone we know?"

"Someone we *thought* we knew," Nancy corrected. "Are you ready for this, Ned? It's Mr. Tremain. He confessed everything. He tried to murder Shannon, thinking she was Angela, and

I'm sure he's been slowly poisoning Angela's mother for the fortune he'll inherit from Mrs. Tremain if Angela dies before she turns twenty-one. He was about to kill me, too!"

His jaw dropped. "You've got to be kidding!"

"See for yourself," Nancy said. "I left him lying on the pier."

Ned raced to the edge of the bluff and looked down. "Well, he's not there now."

Nancy ran to his side and discovered that Ned was right.

Howard Tremain had disappeared!

Chapter

Fifteen

I NEVER THOUGHT he'd come to so soon. We can't let him get away!" Nancy cried. "We have to find him!"

"That shouldn't be too hard. He can't have gone very far." Ned scowled. "And when we *do* find him, am I ever going to enjoy punching his lights out!"

They dashed down the path, but when they got to the beach, the only living things in sight were the gulls that wheeled high overhead or perched on the pilings of the pier. It took Nancy and Ned only a few minutes to realize that there was no place for anyone to hide on that stretch of rocky, barren shore. There was no sign of Howard Tremain. He seemed to have vanished into thin air.

"I don't understand it," Nancy muttered.

"Where can he have gone? He couldn't have come up the path or we would have seen him."

"You got me." Ned turned around to look back at the bluff. "You know, Nan, I just noticed something. There's more than one way to get down here." He pointed to several other paths. "Tremain might have taken one of those, then doubled back to get his car."

"True, but if he did, it wouldn't do him any good," Nancy said. "After I knocked him out, I took his keys."

Ned suddenly slapped his forehead. "Keys! Oh, wow!"

"What's the matter?"

"I just remembered that I left the keys to the Corvette in the ignition!" he groaned. "Tremain could be on his way to the Islip airport by now, and if he makes it to that jet of his, he's out of here, free and clear!"

Nancy knew that Ned was right. "Let's hurry. Maybe it's not too late," she said. "Even though he had a head start, he can't be moving very fast. He hit the pier like a ton of bricks when I threw him, so he still has to be pretty groggy!"

She sprinted for the bluff and raced up the slope with Ned close behind her. They reached the top just in time to see Howard Tremain climbing into the red Corvette.

He saw them, too.

For one horrible moment his mad, blazing

eyes burned into Nancy's, and the hatred she saw there froze her to the spot.

Nancy watched as he revved the powerful engine. But he didn't try to escape by heading for the main road as she had expected. Instead, he turned the wheel of the Corvette and headed straight for Nancy and Ned.

"Look out!" Ned yelled.

He dived at Nancy, wrapping his arms around her waist, and flung her aside just in the nick of time. The car shot past them, teetered for a fraction of a second on the brink of the cliff, then plunged down the slope, pitching wildly from side to side. As it shuddered to a stop on the rocks below, a patrol car pulled up with lights flashing and siren wailing.

Two officers leaped out and came over to Nancy and Ned. "Okay, where's the perpetrator?" one of them asked.

Ned pointed to the beach. "His car went over the cliff when he tried to run us down just now."

The first policeman radioed for an ambulance, then ran down the path to check on the driver of the Corvette.

"Hang on a minute, kid!" The other officer scowled at Ned suspiciously. "That doesn't add up. According to the report we got, the guy was unconscious. If you knocked him out, how was he able to drive a car?"

"He didn't stay unconscious for long," Ned replied. "And for the record, *I* didn't knock him out. My friend here did."

The officer stared at Nancy. *"You* did?"

"What can I say?" She shrugged modestly, "When I threw him, he hit his head on the pier. It was self-defense, officer. Mr. Tremain was going to kill me."

"Are you talking about *Howard* Tremain, the millionaire who owns Soundview?" he asked, astonished.

Nancy nodded. "That's right. He couldn't let me live after I found out that he was the one who attacked Shannon Mulcahey last night— and why."

"Now, hold it right there, young lady!" the officer blustered. "Do you actually expect me to believe that a respectable citizen like Howard Tremain could be capable of attempted murder?"

Nancy looked him straight in the eye. "Yes, I do, because it's the truth. And that's not all. Once I was out of the way, Mr. Tremain planned to dispose of his stepdaughter and his wife as well. He told me so himself." Suddenly she realized that the recorder had been running ever since she began talking with Sean, and now she took it out of her jacket pocket and held it up. "It's all right here on this tape!"

"It is, huh?" The officer looked at Nancy with

new respect. "I guess you'd better tell me the whole story from the very beginning, miss."

So Nancy did.

That part was easy, but breaking the news to Angela and her mother was one of the hardest things Nancy had ever done.

Luckily, Rafe was there when she and Ned returned to Soundview that evening. He sat on the couch between Angela and her mother, with his arms around them.

Nancy slowly began to describe the events of the past few hours: her conversation with Sean, her plan to visit Rocky Point, and finally her conversation and life-threatening encounter with Howard Tremain. She carefully recounted how he had plotted to murder Angela and her mother to secure the Chamberlain fortune for his own purposes.

"I don't know what to say to you. I'm sorry, Angela, Mrs. Tremain. I'm sorry for all that has happened. I'm just relieved you both managed to escape Mr. Tremain's horrible plans for you." Nancy looked from her friend to Mrs. Tremain and could barely stand the pain in their eyes.

"Nancy, there's nothing to be sorry about." Trembling violently, Felicia Tremain covered her face with her hands. "This whole dreadful thing was my fault. I never should have married

Howard, but after Gordon died, I simply couldn't cope. I was so terribly lonely, and Howard was always *there,* helping me get through that awful time. I didn't love him, but I was so weak, and he seemed so strong and safe. . . . How wrong I was!" She turned to Angela, her eyes filled with tears. "Can you ever forgive me for putting your life in danger, darling?"

"There's nothing to forgive, Mother," Angela said wearily. "There was no way you could have guessed how sick Howard was, any more than I could. He fooled everyone."

Nancy grimaced. "Including me."

"Me, too," Ned added.

"But not for long," Mrs. Tremain said. "You saw through him just in time, and you risked your lives to save ours. How can I ever thank you?"

"By getting well as fast as you can," Nancy replied, forcing a smile. "That's also the best Christmas present you can give all of us."

Rafe put his hand on Felicia Tremain's. "And the best wedding present as well!"

Over the following days, Nancy and Ned did their best to help Angela and her mother recover from the shock of Howard Tremain's treachery. Rafe hardly ever left Angela's side. They had postponed their wedding until New Year's Day, and Christmas at Soundview passed quietly.

Nancy's tape of Mr. Tremain's confession, added to the vial of arsenic the police found in their search of the house, proved his guilt beyond a shadow of a doubt. He had been taken to the county prison hospital, where he was recuperating from the injuries he'd sustained when his car went over the cliff at Rocky Point. It was just a matter of time before he'd really be paying for his crimes.

On the afternoon of New Year's Day, a very small, select group gathered in the drawing room at Soundview to witness the marriage of Angela Chamberlain and Raphael Marino. Aside from the servants and Judge Galvin, who was to perform the ceremony, only seven people had been invited, including Mr. and Mrs. Freeman. Like the Freemans, the other two couples had been close friends of Gordon and Felicia Chamberlain. Along with Nancy, Ned, and Rafe, they had offered badly needed comfort and support to Felicia and Angela since Howard Tremain's arrest.

The seventh guest was Carson Drew. The Steinbeck case had ended with a verdict in favor of his client, and Mr. Drew arrived at Soundview on New Year's Eve. Nancy had kept him posted by phone on all that was happening, and when Angela's mother requested that he give the bride away, he readily agreed.

Shortly before four o'clock when the ceremony was scheduled to begin, Nancy came into Angela's bedroom, wearing the red velvet gown her friend had made. As she watched Felicia Tremain fasten a strand of pearls around her daughter's slender throat in front of the full-length mirror, she knew that their nightmare was finally over. Although Mrs. Tremain's health was steadily improving, she was still thin and frail. But the long, softly draped lavender gown she wore was very becoming to her. Her amethyst jewelry echoed the color of her dress, and Nancy could see traces of her former beauty returning.

When Angela turned away from the mirror to face her, Nancy caught her breath. This was the first time she had seen her friend in her bridal gown and veil, and the effect was dazzling.

"Angela, you look fantastic!" she exclaimed.

Smiling tremulously, Angela said, "Do you really think so?"

Felicia Tremain stroked her daughter's cheek. "You both look absolutely beautiful," she murmured. "Just like a pair of fairy-tale princesses!"

"Except that this particular fairy tale has a

weird kind of twist," Angela said. "The villain turned to be the evil step*father* instead of the wicked stepmother."

Her mother shuddered. "I can't bear to think about it! We have to put all that behind us now, darling. A new year is beginning, and so is a wonderful new life for you and Rafe."

Just then there was a brisk knock on the bedroom door. Nancy heard Ned's voice saying, "Are you about ready in there? The bridegroom's downstairs, and he's starting to get a little antsy."

"We're on our way," Nancy called.

Mrs. Tremain took two dainty nosegays of sweetheart roses from the florist's box on the bed. She handed the white bouquet to Angela and the red one to Nancy, kissed each girl tenderly on the cheek, then opened the door.

Carson Drew and Ned, elegantly handsome in black tuxedos, were waiting to escort them to the drawing room. "I've never seen three lovelier ladies," Mr. Drew said, offering one arm to Angela and the other to her mother.

"My sentiments exactly." Ned smiled at Nancy as she tucked her arm through his. "You look spectacular, Nan!"

She smiled back. "You don't look so bad yourself."

As they followed the others down the hall, Ned said, "I just realized something, Nan. We were going to have a private exchange of Christmas presents, but we haven't had any time to ourselves."

"I know," Nancy said. "Since we've waited this long, why don't we wait a little longer and exchange gifts when we get back to River Heights tomorrow? Today belongs to Angela and Rafe. We can celebrate at home, just the two of us."

"You're on." Ned paused at the top of the staircase and drew Nancy into his arms, murmuring into her ear, "But before we do, how about starting the new year right?"

"Sounds like an excellent plan to me," Nancy whispered as she closed her eyes and raised her lips to his.

Nancy's next case:

Nancy, Bess, and George have been invited to the Stafford Military Academy's gala centennial celebration, a weekend of dining and dancing with good-looking guys in uniform. But the festivities take an ugly and tragic turn when one good soldier—Sergeant Stephanie Grindle—becomes a casualty . . . of murder!

Nancy's escort, Captain Nicholas Dufont, has the potential to be a major distraction. But this case requires all of her attention. Behind the military facade, Stafford is a hotbed of hidden rage and secret scandals. And someone at the academy is on a personal mission: Do *anything* to stop Nancy Drew from uncovering the truth . . . in *Against the Rules,* Case #119 in The Nancy Drew Files™.

Nancy Drew
on Campus™

By Carolyn Keene

Available from Archway Paperbacks

Simon & Schuster Mail Order
200 Old Tappan Rd., Old Tappan, N.J. 07675
Please send me the books I have checked above. I am enclosing $_____ (please add $0.75 to cover the postage and handling for each order. Please add appropriate sales tax). Send check or money order–no cash or C.O.D.'s please. Allow up to six weeks for delivery. For purchase over $10.00 you may use VISA: card number, expiration date and customer signature must be included.

POCKET
BOOKS

Name _____

Address _____

City _____ State/Zip _____

VISA Card # _____ Exp.Date _____

Signature _____ 1127-13